*Commander Kellie and the Superkids*_{SM}

#9

False Identity

Christopher P.N. Maselli

KENNETH
COPELAND
PUBLICATIONS

Unless otherwise noted, all scripture is from the following translations:

The Holy Bible, New International Version © 1973, 1978, 1984 by the International Bible Society. Used by permission of Zondervan Publishing House.

International Children's Bible, New Century Version, © 1986, 1988 by Word Publishing, Dallas Texas 75039. Used by permission.

*Commander Kellie and the Superkids*_{SM} is a registered servicemark of Heirborne_{TM}.

Based on the characters created by Kellie Copeland Kutz, Win Kutz, Susan Wehlacz and Loren Johnson.

False Identity

ISBN 1-57562-784-1   30-0909

09 08 07 06 05 04   6 5 4 3 2 1

Kenneth Copeland Publications
Fort Worth, Texas 76192-0001

For more information about Kenneth Copeland Ministries, call 1-800-600-7395 or visit www.kcm.org.

**To Rick Nunez, my fellow
children's minister.**

Contents

Yo Superkid!

Hey, my name is Rapper Rapfield and what happened to me recently was more earthshaking than I ever expected. You see, it all began when I found myself in the last place I expected (or wanted) to be—the undercity caverns of the Vipers.

The Vipers are a gang I belonged to when I was younger—before Commander Kellie and the Superkids helped me out. Now I live at Superkid Academy with Commander Kellie, Paul, Missy, Valerie and Alex. We have adventures together in God all the time. But through a wild circumstance, I ended up housed with the Vipers again.

I knew I had to get out. I knew I wasn't a Viper anymore. The problem was, the rest of the Vipers weren't so convinced of that...and honestly, maybe I wasn't either. If I hadn't discovered...well, you'll see. It took finding out a few things to get me through this one.

Check it out!

Rapper

False Identity

Deep in the heart of the city, underneath the concrete streets and steel skyscrapers, the buzz of electricity crackled and a ceiling light flickered. A soft cloth was torn away from Rapper's eyes.

The young Superkid blinked and squinted into the blackness, the light paining him. He couldn't see much. The dank odor sent a chill of recognition down his spine. He had honestly believed he would never have to smell this place again. But here he was, breathing in its odor. He didn't have to see to know he was at least 100 feet underground, in one of the man-made caves under the city. It wasn't part of the sewage system, but judging by the scum that lived inside, that would be hard to prove.

This was the terrible place where Rapper had spent the four hardest years of his life: challenging, fighting, warring. It hadn't changed much. At the moment it almost felt as though he'd never left...but his heart bore witness that he had.

As his eyes adjusted, Rapper could finally see a young boy kneeling in front of him, grinning. With a small, remote-controlled key, he popped open Rapper's wrist constraints. They fell to the ground.

Rapper recognized this guy. He had olive skin, short, black hair and wore a lightweight, dark-brown jacket. The jacket contained the gear he used for survival. Laser-slicers, electronic devices and other items—whatever the group discovered was necessary.

The boy's chocolate-brown eyes were wide under the dim light as he thrust his hand forward in welcome. Rapper shook his hand unenthusiastically. It was chilly and rough.

"Rapper!" he shouted louder than necessary, letting his hand go. "Welcome back!"

Instinctively, Rapper reached up to the back of his neck and rubbed his skin. With his finger, he traced the thin scar that ran from his hairline to the bottom of his neck. Memories seemed to stir upon his touch.

"We noticed your mark of loyalty is gone—but we can arrange for that to be reapplied. So, you gonna rap for me, rad?"

Rapper pulled his hand forward, habitually, and scratched through his short, spiked, brown hair. *Of all the places he could have ended up...*

"No...not right now," he replied. Then, "Is that you, Squealer?"

The boy threw out his arms to either side, glad for

the recognition.

"He remembers his old friend!" he shouted. Rapper remembered him all right—Squealer got his name because he talked in a high-pitched voice. He also held the name because he was often known to "squeal" on others. Ah, memories.

What am I doing here? Rapper wondered.

Squealer slipped the remote control into one of his jacket pockets. He stood up, exposing his bare legs, dark shorts and black athletic shoes.

"You, my friend, were hard to find."

Rapper scratched his arm. Being in the underground lair again made his skin feel like a hundred daddy longlegs were using it as a jogging trail. "I didn't know anyone was looking for me," he said.

"Yessir," Squealer responded. "And you weren't easy to catch, either."

"The last thing I remember, I was on a mission with Paul. Where's Paul?"

"You mean the tall guy with the bump on the back of his head?"

"He didn't have a—oh."

"He'll be fine. Never knew what hit him. We left him where we found him. We only wanted you."

"How long have I been out?"

"About a day. But I took care of you." Squealer threw his left arm around Rapper's shoulders as Rapper stood up. "Hey, what are rads for?"

"I don't get it," Rapper admitted. "Why would you want me back? You know I've changed."

Squealer tugged on Rapper's royal-blue Superkid uniform. "Well, the outside of you has changed, but I'm willing to bet the inside is still the same."

"That's a bet you'll lose."

"We'll see..." Squealer paused for a long moment and then added, "Python, our leader, was captured by the Claws. You, rad, with all your history here and your 'Superkid' training, have been elected to lead a movement to rescue him."

"What?!"

Squealer just smiled.

Rapper added, "Look, I'm not going to do it. Forget it. This life—this gang life—isn't a part of who I am anymore."

"Right," Squealer muttered. Then he looked at Rapper with absolute conviction. "You'll do it," he said as if those three words explained everything. Rapper huffed. He had no idea how he was going to get out of this.

Squealer slapped Rapper on his shoulder, promising to

return a little later. He wiggled the pinky of his right hand—a common Viper greeting symbolizing a snake's flickering tongue.

"Have a look around," he offered. Rapper shook his head. In the back of his mind, he always thought he might end up visiting this place again sooner or later...*but why couldn't it be later?*

As Squealer exited the small room, Rapper's eye was drawn to the back of the young man's neck, just below his hairline. Drawn there in deep olive green and black was the picture of a coiled snake, his bright-red, forked tongue sticking out of his mouth. And placed between the serpent's eyes was a pair of angry, menacing eyebrows in the shape of a distinct "V" for "Vipers."

Rapper shivered.

Now alone, Rapper took a few cautious steps forward. It had been four years, but not four *quick* years. No, it had been four *long* years. It was hard for Rapper to clearly remember the last time he was part of the Viper's gang life. It was now awkward to him. At the age of 4, he was one of the youngest recruits the Vipers had ever had—and they had been a large part of his life until he was 8 years old. Then *God* happened.

That's when things sped up. Rapper had made Jesus his

Lord his final year of being a Viper. He didn't feel right about being in the gang anymore, but he didn't think he could get out. Then the unthinkable happened. Rapper's older brother was killed. And Rapper knew he *had* to get out. Rapper thanked God daily that his mother contacted the police and they led Rapper to Superkid Academy, one of the many organizations that worked to help "street kids" (as they were sometimes called). They helped Rapper get out *fast.* The next thing he knew, he was living for God every day. He was going on missions to help others. He was sometimes nothing short of amazed at what God had done with a young "street kid."

Rapper stepped into the awesome Vipers' cavern. The main arena was about the size of half a football field. Painted wide in the center of the place, on the floor, was the angry Vipers' symbol—the snake in all its viciousness. Surrounding it, the nearly 100-foot, domed walls were formed of hard cement, splattered with graffiti. Along the walls, up high, down low and in the middle were nooks, crevices and crannies leading to hidden rooms, long tunnels and escape routes. It was all part of the gigantic underground system that the city gangs occupied.

Nearly 30 years ago, most gangs had been driven underground by the legal system. Now they were known as "undercity" gangs. Their divisions were rarely by race or lifestyle. Instead they owned territories and were known by their "crime style" and method of financial gain. Even though much had changed throughout the years, most of their tactics remained the same. Violence, fear, intimidation and slander filled the gang environment. Sadly, Rapper knew, the Vipers were no different.

The Vipers were known for their superior laser-slicing. (Rapper was pretty good with a laser-slicer himself, though most people never knew it.) Stealing new technology was their main source of financial gain. It was nothing to be proud of, for sure, but it was how they defended their territory and protected their fellow "rads." Rapper snarled. "Defense and protection" was what they called it. The reality? It was nothing more than fear.

Rapper looked up at the intricate, steel catwalk system, crisscrossing throughout the cavern. Painted midnight black, portions of it were almost invisible against the dark, coarse ceiling. It stretched the full length of the room, connecting one tiny outlet to another. A whoosh of warm air hit Rapper as a Serfsled zipped through the air with a Viper on top.

Serfsleds were air-powered vehicles that defied the laws of gravity. They looked like 5-foot glass, oval pancakes with a set of vintage motorcycle seats, a windshield and a pair of handlebars on top. Rapper used to love to fly them. As one shot through the air above him, he saw the Vipers' mascot snake painted on the underside. He frowned.

Wham!

From out of nowhere, Rapper was knocked to the pavement. The bright, yellow lights hanging from the cavern ceiling blurred before him as he tried to find his attacker.

He didn't have to look too far.

"Umph!" Rapper coughed as a knee pressed into his gut. A lanky young man with short, fiery-red hair and rough stubble on his chin brought his face close to Rapper's. His warm breath rolled off Rapper's cheek.

"Your call, your crew!" he shouted through clenched teeth. Rapper stayed silent, looking at him eye-to-eye. "Your call, your crew!" he shouted again.

"Rapper's my call," Rapper responded slowly and coolly. "And I no longer belong to a crew."

"Zat right? Then you, rad, are tressin'." He threw his fist at Rapper's face. A split second before impact, Rapper jerked his body sideways and threw his opponent off balance. The young man was older and taller, but Rapper was faster. He flipped him over and ended up on top. Anger filled the string bean's eyes as he gazed up at Rapper. His dark-red eyebrows made his gray eyes look sunken back behind his stark, white skin.

"I'm not tressin', rad," Rapper said slowly and cooly. "The Vipers brought me here. Now what's your call and crew?"

The boy remained silent.

Rapper raised his eyebrows.

"My call is Strike First. My crew is the Vipers. And I don't know nothing about you being brought here by no one."

"Rad, we need to sign you up for grammar school."

"You dissin' me?"

"No, I'm not. 'Strike First,' huh? How'd you get that name?" Rapper smiled.

"You have a real attitude problem, rad."

"*I* do? Hey, I'm just looking for whoever's in charge now that Python's been captured."

Strike First cracked a daring smile. Then with an unexpected move, he pulled his leg aside and kicked back at Rapper's. The Superkid was caught by surprise as the Viper flipped him over and pressed his shoulders to the floor.

"You lookin' for the man in charge?" Strike First snarled. "Well...you've found him."

* * *

"What's with the fancy get-up?" Strike First asked, flicking his finger on Rapper's Superkid wings badge.

Rapper looked down at his outfit. It was true: The royal blue color made him stand out compared to the drab browns and blacks the Vipers wore. But he wasn't about to admit that to Strike First. Rapper stood straight. "These are my wings and my colors," he said.

Strike First shook his head mockingly.

Strike First escorted Rapper to the Vipers' Common Room. This "operations room" consisted of a few cabinets, desks, computers and other—mostly stolen—high-tech equipment. It wasn't much more than a hole in the wall, but it served its purpose. As Rapper looked around, he realized, it too, hadn't changed much. Perhaps there were a few more cracks in the graffiti-covered walls than before. And a few more painted snakes. He remembered being in that room often, listening to the leader make rash decisions in an attempt to take revenge on another gang or regain territory.

"So you're a Superkid? I hearda them. You're like a goody-two-shoes group for God, ain'cha?"

"Superkid Academy is the place that saved me from having to live like a criminal with the Vipers," Rapper replied.

Strike First flipped his head in Rapper's direction. "There you go, dissin' us again."

"I'm not disrespecting you," Rapper said emphatically.

"I'm just telling it like it is. Before I became a Christian and met the Superkids, my life was dead. But now I'm alive like never before. Jesus did that for me."

"Save it, rad. We don't need none of that preachin' here."

Rapper couldn't help it. He knew where he had come from—and where he was going. If it hadn't been for Commander Kellie and the Superkids, if he had stayed with the Vipers...he knew he may not even be alive anymore.

Squealer entered the room with two young men.

"Hey, rads! Check it! I've got two new recruits!"

Rapper's face fell as the announcement was made.

Young Squealer held out his olive hands dramatically as he began the introductions.

"This is Jaws, our prize recruit." The mid-sized, lighter-skinned boy nodded in Strike First's direction. "He's a technical whiz who's going to get our servers running like wildfire."

Strike First stared at Jaws rudely and blurted out loud, "What happened to you?"

Hooked from around the back of Jaws' head to the front and covering the entire lower half of his face was a brace. It covered his nostrils, mouth and chin like a leather-and-steel scarf. The skin on his sharp cheekbones was stretched by the brace. His forehead and bright-green eyes were all that were left to get an idea of his expression. His shoulder-length hair was bleached white and drawn back in a ponytail.

"I've had to hold my own," he simply responded. His voice reverberated through a computerized voice activator in his brace. Rapper could only imagine what he must have been through.

"And this is Newbie," Squealer continued. "He's joining us as a newcomer to the wonderful life of the undercity. He has no refined skills yet, but he's more than willing to learn."

Newbie nodded. He was a mid-sized, dark-skinned boy with innocent brown eyes and a thin mouth. His hair was cut close. Rapper closed his eyes and shook his head.

Strike First eyed them skeptically and inquired, "Have they both been through a background check?"

"They're clean," Squealer replied. "I wouldn't bring 'em to you if they weren't."

"Welcome to the Vipers," Strike First said. He wiggled the pinky finger of his right hand at them. The two new boys returned the greeting obediently.

Rapper slapped a metal table he was leaning against. "That's it?" he asked. He moved over to Newbie. "How old are you?"

"Nine," he answered. Rapper shook his head and

moved to Jaws.

"And you?"

"Eleven," he responded.

Rapper whirled around to Strike First. "Nine and 11—did you hear that?! These are *kids*. They don't belong in gangs."

From behind Rapper, Squealer spoke up. "And how old were you when you first came to the Vipers?"

Rapper remembered the incident all too well. It had been eight years ago…

* * *

Robert wiped a single tear from his eye, but tried to keep as quiet as he could. He didn't want his older brother in the upper bunk to know he was crying.

"Hey, Robert, you OK?"

Robert frowned. Great.

"I'm fine," he lied. There was a long pause. But since his brother was awake, Robert had to ask. "Where do you think Dad is tonight?"

His brother let out a long sigh. "It has been two years, Robert. If I've told you once, I've told you a thousand times: He's not coming back."

"But it's Christmas. He could've called us this year."

Robert's brother leaned over the top of the bunk and looked down at him. The orange glow from their small night light reflected on his face.

"Look, I know this is hard for you to understand since you're only 4, but our family is never going to be like it was."

"Why not?"

"Because it's not."

"That's no answer."

"It's the truth."

Robert had no response to that.

"Look," his brother, Nicholas, finally offered, "I met some guys today. They're in this group and they said they'd like me to join them. I'm thinking about it."

"What do you mean?" Robert wondered.

"I mean I may have found a way for us to not have it so hard with Dad gone. They said they'd show me how to take care of myself...and my family."

Another long pause.

"Hey, Nick, you think I can come, too?"

"You're a little young."

"I am not. I can do anything. I wanna help."

"All right," Nicholas responded, dropping out of sight and leaning back on his pillow. "I'll ask them."

"I'm not too young, you will see! I'm as tough as any-one can be," Robert rapped.

Nicholas chuckled. "Hey, brother, you keep rhyming like

that and we may just have to start calling you 'Rapper.'"

* * *

"I gotta get outta here," Rapper said to the others, shaking his head. "I don't belong here."

"This rad is more trouble than he's worth," Strike First said to Squealer, angling his thumb at Rapper. "You were wrong. He's not gonna do us any good."

"Thank you!" Rapper said, heading for the door. "I'm going home."

"You *are* home, rad," Squealer said, blocking the door.

"I'm *not* home! I don't belong here. You heard your *leader.*" Rapper pushed past Squealer, exiting the room.

He hadn't gone two more steps before Squealer threw in the clincher. "Rapper, you gave your word to Python...in blood."

Rapper froze.

"What's this?" Strike First piped up.

Squealer explained. "When Rapper joined us way back when, he was Python's 'sipe. Python took him under his wing and taught him everything he knew. He was next in line to be our leader. In exchange for that position, Rapper gave his word—in blood—that if Python ever needed help, he'd be there for him. Now you're trying to skirt your responsibility, aren't you, *Superkid?*"

Rapper felt his mouth go dry. Everything Squealer said was true. Rapper had given his word in blood. And to the Vipers, that meant everything. It was the strongest kind of promise one gang member could give to another.

"It's true," Rapper whispered. He slowly turned around and re-entered the room in a daze. "But you can't be serious. I'm...I'm just different now. I want to help Python, but I'm not a Viper anymore. My Superkid manual says in 2 Corinthians 5:17 that when Jesus comes into your life, old things are passed away—everything becomes new. I'm not the same person."

"So you're not going to keep your promise?" Squealer asked. "Your blood promise?" Strike First was still frowning.

"What do I have to do?" Rapper asked softly. He wasn't about to cross the line...but he couldn't go back on his word either. He *had* made a promise. And now Squealer was calling on it.

Squealer walked over and put a hand on Rapper's shoulder. "As I mentioned earlier, you're going to lead us on a rescue mission to get Python."

"Since when did *he* get the juice?" Strike First spat. "And who are *you* to give him the juice?"

Squealer held out his hands in defense. "Hey, rad,

Rapper's the 'sipe. That gives him the juice, he has the power. It puts him in charge."

"I'm in charge!" Strike First shouted.

"Not any longer," Rapper said coolly. "Now I've got the juice."

"The juice?!" Strike First shouted. "You ain't got the juice! You ain't got respect for the Vipers! You come in your flashy uniform actin' like that. You don't even got a mark of loyalty no more! You ain't nothin'! *Nothin'!"*

Rapper kept his composure. "Perhaps you missed it, but Squealer just said I'm the 'sipe."

Strike First shoved his pointed finger in the air as if he wanted to say something more, but then decided not to. Finally he said, "Fine. You be the 'sipe." He turned to Squealer. "But when his juice runs out, nobody better ask what happened. 'Cuz I'm tellin' you now: He's gonna turn this rescue into a disaster."

"We'll see," Rapper said. He looked at Newbie and Jaws who were staring at him with wrinkled foreheads. "We'll see."

27

The long passageway looked like any other cement-walled, cramped corridor in the undercity. Nonetheless, this one chilled Rapper to the bone. He knew around the next corner was the lair of the Claws—archenemies of the Vipers. As far back as he could remember, Vipers talked nasty about this enemy group. They were mean, criminal and determined. This, of course, made them an even match for the Vipers.

They, like the Vipers, used technology as their primary weapon. Though instead of laser-slicers, most Claws wore a flexible, skintight glove with an electric patch woven into the knuckles. When their fists were closed, the electricity flowed. The Claws got their name because when their gloves made contact, electricity arched from them, resembling a claw.

Also, like the Vipers, the Claws made a living stealing technology. They were a smart lot...and that made the mission to rescue Python all the more difficult.

Rapper felt tired at the midnight hour. Kneeling with the rest, he peeked around the corner. Squealer, at his side, jerked him back with a chilly hand as he squealed, "Hey, rad, you tryin' to get yourself killed?"

"That wasn't my plan, no," Rapper whispered back.

Strike First, rising up behind them, mumbled. "He's gonna get all nine of us killed."

"Quiet," Rapper retorted.

"You told us we couldn't bring any weapons. How stupid is that?"

Rapper leaned in toward Strike First. He spoke soft, but firm. "No one said this was gonna be easy. But as long as Python is alive, what he says goes. And he made me his 'sipe, which makes me the leader when he's out. Now are you gonna follow the leader or not?"

Strike First shook his head, rolling his sunken eyes. "Whatever."

Rapper let it drop. "Squealer," he addressed, "I need your input here. How do you think we ought to approach this?"

Strike First's mouth dropped open. In hushed tones, he said, "What?! You don't have a plan?!" Squealer looked equally surprised.

"No, I don't have a plan," Rapper responded defensively. "I was thrown into this whole thing only a few hours ago and I haven't had much time to think—or pray."

"Religion Boy doesn't know what to do without his comfortable Superkid suit on," Strike First mocked. Rapper shook his head. He had traded in his Superkid outfit for standard Viper wear. He figured the dark, denim shorts, brown jacket, olive T-shirt and black athletic shoes would serve him better in the tunnels.

"All right," Strike First finally gave in. His dark chin hairs bobbed up and down as he spoke. "Here's what I say: Let's send one rad ahead of us to keep the hallway quiet. Down the way about 6 meters is another curve and then the opening to the Claws' domain. Our rad can take out the guard Claw and then the rest of us can rush in. Rapper, you and Squealer find Python. I'll lead the rest in a rumble. Who knows? Maybe we can take a few out along the way."

"Whoa-whoa-whoa!" Rapper said, waving his hands. "Nobody's taking anybody *out. Here's* the plan. One person goes ahead and quietly captures the guard Claw." Rapper pulled out the blindfold he had been wearing only a couple hours earlier. "This goes in his mouth and use a wrist constraint on his arms. Meanwhile, the rest of us sneak in and search for Python. When we find him, we'll get him out without a word. I want everyone back here in 10 minutes."

"You really think that's going to work?" wondered Squealer.

"It's a stupid plan," Strike First put in his two cents.

"You have a better one?"

"I gave you my plan."

"So your answer is 'no.'"

Strike First bit his lip. Rapper addressed Squealer.

"All right, rad, you said there are six others behind us?"

"That's right."

"Who do you think is sneaky enough to get to the Claw guard without being seen?"

Squealer thought for a moment. He rubbed his lips with his finger. "I think Newbie could do it. He's pretty small."

"OK, good. I—did you just say 'Newbie'?" Rapper couldn't believe his ears.

"Yeah..."

"You guys are nuts, aren't you?" Rapper had to ask. "He doesn't even know what he's doing and yet you invited him into a dangerous situation!"

"Jaws is here, too," Squealer pointed out.

"C'mon, rad," Strike First said heartlessly, "you know as well as we do that we need a buffer."

Rapper felt himself clenching his fist. *"A buffer? Is that why you invited them to be Vipers? So you could let them get beat up to save your own neck?"*

"What?! It's not like this is the first time! This is war!" Strike First shouted in a hush.

Rapper put his finger in Strike First's face. "God will

be your judge," he said, punching every word. Strike First didn't move a muscle.

Rapper dropped his hand. "This has got to stop. This fighting has got to stop." He motioned to the group behind him. "Newbie! Jaws! Where are you? Come up here!" From the back of the group, the boys emerged.

When they reached the front, Rapper put one hand on each of their right arms. "Guys, I want you to stick with me, you understand? No heroics today." The boys nodded.

Strike First nabbed Rapper's blindfold and handed it to a boy behind him. He asked him to go ahead and do as Rapper had ordered: Sneak up on the Claw guard and muffle him. When he had done so, he was to send a signal to the rest of the group. The boy agreed and took off fearlessly, yet quietly, down the tunnel.

The group sat silently together as they waited. Rapper prayed softly under his breath.

Having Newbie and Jaws along threw a wrench in the plan. Thoughts of protecting the boys flooded his mind. He knew he had to rescue Python—he knew he had to keep his promise.

But Newbie was just an innocent kid...and Jaws' obvious brace just showed how much he needed help holding his ground. Rapper felt responsible.

What if something were to happen to either one? They weren't even teenagers yet! Rapper rubbed his eyelids. *He* wasn't even a teenager yet. *Great.* What were *any* of them doing getting ready to enter a fight like this? Battle after battle, give and take. In the scope of eternity, all it did was hurt people. The fighting had to stop.

Rapper knew he didn't belong here. This wasn't him anymore. He was different. But he had given his word. Silently, he vowed to get away from the gang as soon as his word was fulfilled.

Newbie rubbed the back of his neck. It was a gesture Rapper recognized. He grabbed the boy's arm and pulled him forward. Suddenly he saw a splash of color shine from beneath Newbie's hairline. It was a tattoo...a Viper's mark of loyalty.

"How did he get this?" Rapper asked Squealer in a hushed voice.

"I asked for it," Newbie volunteered. "I want to be a Viper."

"Why?" Rapper asked.

The young boy's forehead wrinkled. "What do you mean?"

"What I mean is, has anyone told you what gang life is like?"

"It's gotta be better than the life I have."

"That's what I thought, too," Rapper responded. "I found out I was wrong."

Newbie twisted his lip. He didn't understand. Rapper knew he wouldn't. Not yet.

"When you need to," Rapper whispered, "you can get out—and you can get that removed like I did."

"Hey, rad," Strike First interjected. "Don't be tellin' him lies. Once he's in, he's in." Strike First looked directly at Newbie's eyes. "We're loyal to each other. You don't want to leave."

"And what happens if he does?" Rapper challenged.

"Don't ask questions like that," Squealer returned.

"He can't remove that symbol anyway," Strike First said flippantly. "We don't put them on like we used to. They're permanent now."

Rapper looked at the Viper curiously.

"We use a new process," Squealer explained. "It's a special ink that actually becomes one with your skin—it's safer, too. Your blood repels the ink so you can't get contaminated. That was a problem for a while. One gang—the Stings—were using it as a weapon. Can't do that anymore with this new process. But once it's on, it's on."

Rapper looked at Newbie. "I'm sorry," he said.

Newbie shrugged. Rapper peeked over to see if Jaws had a tattoo. It didn't look like he did yet. His brace was in the way, though, so Rapper wasn't sure.

Beep-beep!

Strike First looked at his watch.

"That's it!" he reported. "He's through. Let's go!"

Rapper, Strike First, Squealer, Newbie, Jaws and three others crawled their way through the cramped tunnel. Rapper was pleased to see that the boy they had sent ahead had done his job as Rapper had asked. He had simply muffled the Claw guard and bound him.

Rapper exited the hole and entered into the edge of the Claws' lair. He was surprised at how much it looked like the Vipers' lair. The walls, floor and ceiling were formed with the same, jagged, gray cement. The Claws didn't use catwalks, Rapper noticed, but ropes hung from the ceiling in all directions, some dangling, others tied at several points. There appeared to be no pulleys or Serfsleds, and that puzzled Rapper. He couldn't figure out how they moved around the cave without them. He frowned. As he waited for the other Vipers to exit the tunnel, he realized how quiet it was in the Claws' hide-out. Sure, it was just a few hours after midnight...but even the smallest gang usually had more than one guard around.

Newbie must have noticed this, too.

"Maybe they're out on a mission like us," he observed, whispering.

"If so, this'll be easier than we thought," Rapper said.

SMACK!

Rapper whirled around. The guard was crumpled on the floor. Rapper looked up and saw Strike First standing over him.

"What?!" Strike First asked with his hands out in surrender. "I just knocked him out."

"I wanted to ask him a few questions," Rapper said irritably.

"He would have lied anyway," Strike First growled.

"All right," Rapper addressed the group. He decided now wasn't the time to argue with Strike First. "As far as we know, the Claws have only three prison rooms. Python has to be in one. Let's divide into groups of three—and each group will go to one of the prison rooms. The fourth group will stay here, guard our escape route and signal us if there's trouble. Got it?"

The group nodded.

"Check back here in 10 minutes. Let's go!" he whispered, full of energy.

Instantly he grabbed Newbie and Jaws. "You're coming with me," he ordered. Strike First took another group and

Squealer took another. They each broke off in a different direction.

* * *

Rapper began instinctively praying under his breath again. "Father God, give me wisdom. Like Ephesians 1:18 says, let the eyes of my heart be enlightened. Thank You, God, for Your protection."

Rapper motioned to Newbie and Jaws when he finally found the cubbyhole entrance he had been looking for. It was dark inside, but a soft, blue light near the ceiling made it bright enough. Rapper felt like a rat seeking out cheese at the end of a maze. He couldn't see beyond the next wall and while he was hoping for the prize to be around the corner, he expected to find nothing but more walls.

"This is exciting!" Newbie whispered, exhilarated. Rapper shook his head.

"Don't get too comfortable," he responded. "We're not out yet."

Jaws stayed quiet and followed behind. His bright, green eyes were solid and searching. Even though he was new to the Vipers, Rapper could tell he was an experienced boy. It was comforting to know he was watching their back. Still...when Rapper found a moment, he was set on talking both Jaws and Newbie out of staying with the

Vipers. A gang was the *last* place they needed to be.

"There!" Jaws' voice reverberated through his jaw-brace mouthpiece. He was pointing straight ahead. Rapper squinted. There it was. A cell. And one figure inside. Even though the room was a dusty blue, Rapper recognized the figure. It was Python. His shoulders were slumped and his head was down, but it was him. It had been four years, but Rapper remembered Python as a burly, older teenager—the kind of guy who could have been the quarterback on his school's football team.

Rapper thought for a second that he saw a shadow move at the side of the small cavern, near another exit. But the longer he stared, the more he was sure it was just his eyes and the darkness playing tricks on him. The three boys were alone in the room....*This is strange,* thought Rapper.

Stationing Newbie and Jaws as his lookouts, Rapper approached the cage.

"Python!" Rapper whispered.

Nothing.

"Python!" he said a little louder. Hearing his own voice made Rapper uncomfortable. Suddenly the figure stirred. He turned his head slowly and then his mouth dropped.

"Rapper Rapfield?" he mouthed in wonderment. Rapper smiled. He had found him. And he had done it his way—*without* violence. Now all he had to do was get Python out and he could go back to Superkid Academy. His promise would be fulfilled. *Yes.*

"I kept my word," Rapper spoke to Python, feeling about 7 years younger. "I've come to help you."

Python stood, shaking a bit. He was just as Rapper remembered him. Straggly, black hair, black skin, hefty build. He was in his standard Viper gear, and he looked weak—like he hadn't had any food to eat for a while. He walked to the front of the cage.

Rapper ran his fingers over the electronic keypad on the door. "It'll take us just a few minutes with our tools."

"Rad," he addressed Rapper, pointing a dark finger. "There—down the hall. Fourth room on the left."

"What?" Rapper asked. "That's where the code is?"

"Yes. Behind a picture of the city…in a box in the wall."

Jaws offered, "I'll get it." Rapper nodded.

As Jaws quietly scuffled away, Rapper held Python's eyes. Neither of them said a word.

A few moments later, Jaws returned, an object in his hand. He handed it to Rapper.

"What's this?" Rapper looked at the item. It looked like two pens molded together, one atop the other. The bottom one was hard rubber, the top sleek metal. Rapper took it by the rubber end.

"That's what was in the box," Jaws replied.

"Squeeze it," Python whispered.

Rapper felt a scream go off inside him. A warning. But it didn't make any sense. "Is this a weapon?" Rapper asked. "I don't fight with the weapons of this world."

The Viper leader cracked a thin smirk. "You haven't seen anything like this before," he said. "It's a prototype the Claws have developed. Try it."

Rapper looked at the object again, then over at Newbie, then Jaws. They weren't looking at him. They were watching the exits. Rapper looked back at the object.

"Go ahead," Python pressed. "You'll need it to get me out of here."

Rapper let out a long breath. They hadn't come this far to turn back now.

His mouth was as dry as cotton. It had been a long time since he had held a weapon in his hand. He moved it back and forth in front of his eyes.

Slowly, carefully, Rapper squeezed the rubbery grip. He could feel the rubber under the tips of his fingers give way to a lever underneath. Then he heard a "click!" like a lighter igniting and instantly the metal glowed a bright yellow-white.

Rapper's eyes grew wide and Newbie and Jaws turned around to look at the brilliant source of light.

"What is this?" Rapper asked.

"They call it an Electroblade," Python whispered, smiling. The light from the blade cast an eerie glow on his pale, white teeth. "The Claws have developed an incredible technology, Rapper. The electricity flowing through that blade is strong and condensed. Anything the blade touches is ripped apart at the atomic level."

Rapper stared at the blade.

"Touch it to these bars," Python ordered. Rapper slowly turned, never taking his eyes off the blade. The weapon seemed to vibrate in his hand like a vacuum-cleaner handle...only it was nearly silent. In the quiet darkness, Rapper could hear only a light hum of electricity.

Python gestured and Rapper touched the Electroblade to one of the thick, steel bars.

Pzzzzzt! Pow! The electricity surrounding the blade cracked against the bar and sparks flew. Each boy's eyes were wide with amazement. *It was actually slicing through the bar!*

The blade sizzled all the way through and Rapper pulled it back up. He turned it around in front of his face.

"This-this-this-this is...wow..."

"Never seen anything like it, huh, rad?" Python questioned.

"Never."

"And it's small enough to fit in your pocket. Now how 'bout letting me out?"

"Huh? Oh, right!" Rapper said louder than he wanted. He brought the blade down to the keypad on the door and sliced right through it. A few heartbeats later, the entire pad dropped to the ground and Python opened the door.

"I'm FREE!" he shouted with all his might. Rapper, Newbie and Jaws jumped in shock.

"Quiet!" Rapper hushed.

Python shook his head. "What do I have to worry about?" he asked. "The exit's near and I have Rapper back on my side—no one's better with a laser-slicer...or an Electroblade!"

"No!" Rapper shouted back in a harsh whisper. He let his grip loosen on the Electroblade and it went out. "I don't fight that way anymore! I don't fight flesh and blood. I don't fight on my own!"

"Well, you came in here to get me on your own, rad."

Rapper wanted to say something strong and powerful back, but he couldn't think of anything...all he could think was that perhaps Python was right. After all, had he ever *really* asked the Lord what he should do?

"This is the technology we need!" Python broke Rapper's thoughts. He tore the Electroblade out of his hand. He squeezed it and with a click, it was glowing bright. "I want to outfit every Viper with one. We're smarter than the Claws and soon *we'll* be the most-respected gang in the undercity!"

"Wait a second," Rapper interrupted. "Do all the Claws have one of these?"

"No!" Python promised. "This is the prototype, remember? It's the only one. Now it's ours! Ha-ha! The Claws would kill to get this back!"

Rapper took a deep breath. "We've got to get out of here."

The three Vipers and Rapper ran back down the
passageway and into the main arena. Python, being
weak from hunger, slowed them down a bit, but otherwise they made good time. Against Rapper's hopes,
Python still had the Electroblade, bright and glowing.
But there wasn't much he could do about it. Python,
the Vipers' leader, was in charge again. Besides, if
Rapper had his way, he'd be out of the Vipers' territory
by dawn and he wouldn't have to think about this vacant
lifestyle any longer.

From across the huge room, Rapper saw Squealer
waving his arms. He and his group were running toward
them frantically, like they were running from a swarm
of bees.

Something was wrong.

Strike First and his group weren't around yet—had
they already made it to the escape tunnel?

Shhhhhhhhhh...

Shhhhhhhhhh...

Shhhhhhhhhh...

Rapper and the Vipers—including Squealer and his
group—stopped in their tracks. They looked around

curiously as the shushing sound enveloped them. It sounded like a wheeled vehicle driving through the rain...only softer. And a bit...higher.

Jaws looked up and saw it first. His voice cracked as he screamed and without warning a Claw dropped from above and knocked straight into him.

Rapper spun around, looking up in bewilderment as at least 20 Claws came sliding down the angled ropes he had seen earlier. They rode down swiftly and deliberately on hand pulleys. A few hopped ropes along the way, quickly changing course.

Whap! A Claw walloped Rapper in the back. Rapper struck the ground with a thud. He discovered his first thought was wondering why he had made the Vipers leave their weapons so far behind. The Claw who hit him clenched his right fist and his gloved knuckles glowed with electricity.

"No weapon used against me shall defeat me!" Rapper exclaimed, remembering Isaiah 54:17. In defense, he kicked forward, knocking the Claw off his feet. Rapper didn't waste any time. "Vipers! Let's get out of here!" he cried, hoping the others would hear.

Jaws kneed the Claw on him in the stomach and sent him tumbling over. Newbie ran over to help, but was he slid down. It wasn't powerful enough to slice all the way through, but it was enough to weaken the rope. The weight of the Claw ripped the remainder of the rope in half and the boy fell 15 feet to the ground. Rapper nodded.

"Newbie!" Jaws shouted, pointing across the way. Rapper saw the Claw on top of him with his closed fist up in the air. The Claw struck Newbie in the chest, shocking him.

"No!!!" Rapper cried. Running full speed, Rapper shot across the distance between them and smashed full force into the side of the Claw.

"Aaarrrggghhh!"

The two rivals rolled on top of one another and the Claw kicked and punched. Rapper effectively kept away from his closed fist. Rapper smacked his forehead into the other boy's. The boy's head knocked back onto the ground as he lost consciousness. Pain shot through Rapper's skull and he froze in disbelief, realizing the force he had resorted to using. He was mad. He wasn't thinking. He was using self-defense tactics, without even taking time to ask God for help.

"Ohhhhh..." Rapper crawled over to Newbie, who was moaning on the ground. He had a black eye and Rapper imagined he had several broken ribs.

"Why did this have to happen? Why did this have to

caught halfway by another sliding Claw. His knuckles were glowing and he was at least twice Newbie's age and weight.

On their way to the escape tunnel, Squealer and his group held their own.

Rapper turned and gasped. Three Claws—two clenching their free fists and one with a laser-slicer—were heading straight for him. They slid down their ropes so fast Rapper didn't have time to think about what to do next. On instinct, he ducked and closed his eyes.

Fffttaaaapppp! Rapper opened his eyes to see a thick rope stretched out to catch all three Claws in midair flight and sending them thumping to the ground. Rapper was surprised—and thrilled—to see Strike First and his team on each side of the defensive rope. For once, he was glad Strike First was there.

Briefly free, they ran over to help Squealer and his team. A laser-slicer slid over and stopped at Rapper's feet.

"Where's Newbie?!" Rapper cried. Suddenly, another Claw came sliding down toward Jaws. Rapper reached down and grabbed the laser-slicer at his feet. He aimed instinctively, pointing the weapon at the rope. With a press of a button, a small, red laser shot forward and landed behind the Claw's head, directly in the center of the rope happen?" Rapper mumbled. He had tried to help. He thought he could handle protecting the two boys...but he couldn't be in two places at once.

"It'll be all right," Rapper reassured, not quite believing it himself. He knew he had to get the boy to the hospital...but he had to get him out of the Claws' lair first.

Rapper looked over at Squealer, Strike First and the others. He noticed three Vipers were on the ground, knocked out. There were a few motionless Claws, too. The rest had fully retreated. Jaws was near. He looked all right. He stood aside, looking down at the fallen Viper in front of him. Rapper couldn't believe it. It was Python.

Rapper motioned for a couple of the Vipers to help Newbie and then he ran over and fell at Python's side.

"You all right, rad?" Rapper asked, knowing the answer before it was spoken. The Viper leader had several electric burns on his shirt. His voice was raspy. "I think I need to go to the hospital."

Rapper looked up and saw a tear had rolled out of Jaws' eye. "Newbie needs help," Rapper said to Jaws, motioning in Newbie's direction. Jaws got the hint and headed off to help him.

"What happened?" Rapper asked Python. The dark-skinned leader shook his head weakly.

"I was caught off guard," he responded. "I was caught off guard..."

"You'll be all right," Rapper encouraged him. "Just don't fade on me. We'll get you to a hospital."

"Who knows...maybe this is my time." Python groaned.

"Your *time?!* Whoa—nuh-uh. Rad, you're only 19...." Rapper worked to focus his thoughts. He calmed a bit. "Hey, look. Do you know Jesus as your Lord? That's all that matters now. You want to go to heaven, Python?"

Python's eyes were closed.

"Python!"

It was eerily familiar...

* * *

"Nick!"

Rapper rushed to his older brother's side. Nicholas had just hit the ground, splashing into a rain puddle.

Rapper grabbed his brother by the neck and turned his head upright. He could see the edge of the Viper tattoo on the back of his neck. He suddenly found himself hating that tattoo he had once wanted so badly.

Nicholas' chest was moving up and down quickly as he took huge gasps of air.

"You'll be all right," Rapper promised. But somehow he knew that wasn't true. He had heard the shot with his

own two ears. In the dim streetlight, Rapper could only make out a bright, yellow mark on the side of the shooter's hand. A letter...or a symbol...Rapper wasn't sure. All he remembered was seeing it wrapped around that laser weapon. And then he saw the vibrant, red light. His brother fell. And the rival gang member disappeared. Rapper didn't even know which gang had done it. He knew he probably never would.

And it didn't matter.

All that mattered right now was his brother.

"Remember Mom tellin' us about Jesus?" Rapper prompted.

His brother shook his head weakly.

"I believe in Jesus, Nick. You need Him in your heart if you wanna go to heaven. Have you ever asked Him into your heart, Nick?"

His brother's head rolled sideways and his eyes were closing. Rapper grabbed Nicholas' head and patted his cheek.

"Nick! This is important! You have to tell me! I need to know! Did you ever ask Jesus to be your Lord? Just tell me! Please tell me!"

Nick gulped and with his last breath of air he whispered, "I—"

"I should have been there...I should have been there," Rapper whispered as he rode in the ambulance. The hovering vehicle flew through the city streets, gliding on air.

Rapper, Strike First, Squealer and Jaws sat beside Newbie, who lay on a hard cot. They had managed to get him, Python and the others safely out of the Claws' lair. They called a couple of ambulances and got Python, Newbie and another badly hurt boy to the upper city. Python and the other Viper were in a vehicle in front of them. It all happened so fast, Rapper could barely remember what took place. He really thought he could have gotten them in and out of the Claws' lair without any confrontation...without any weapons...without any fighting. Pain rushed through Rapper's mind as he asked God why his plan hadn't worked.

Rapper felt as worn out as Strike First, Squealer and Jaws looked. The surprise attack was more than he had planned for and his injuries were more than he had bar-gained for. But still, it could have been worse. They were all so young. Anger filled Rapper as he looked at Newbie, beaten, bruised and broken. His healing would eventually come, but Rapper knew it would take longer for his beaten, bruised and broken spirit to be healed.

Rapper silently prayed that according to Matthew 10:20 the Holy Spirit would give him just the right words to say. *God, I'm not sure what to say on my own. Let it not be me speaking, but Your Spirit through me.*

Jaws was the one who was willing to help him rescue Newbie and get him on his way to the hospital. The other Vipers were more reluctant. Their trips to the surface were rarely for help...more often they were simply a means to gain more power, more "stuff." This lack of concern for others, too, sparked anger in Rapper.

Strike First and Squealer had agreed to come along— they said it was because they wanted to support their Viper rad. Rapper knew better. He knew they were tagging along to keep an eye on him. As far as they were concerned, he was "back." This, of course, meant he was part of the gang, rather than a *prisoner* of the gang. He knew if he tried to get out there would be a price to pay. But at this point, Rapper didn't care what the consequences might be. He wanted to get ahold of Superkid Academy and get out. Now. He hadn't asked to be a Viper again. He had been forced. Of course, when he left four years ago, he hadn't asked if he could leave. He had just disappeared. He knew as far as Strike First and Squealer were concerned, Superkid Academy had forced him to leave. They felt he belonged with the Vipers—even if Strike First acted as though he hated him. That didn't mean he didn't value him.

Rapper rubbed his face. Everything was muddled in his mind in the wake of the tragedy.

The ambulance came to a whining stop outside the city's main hospital. The back doors swung open and the four boys exited. Two tall medics grabbed the gurney, activated an airlift, and led the floating cot into the hospital.

* * *

Python was behind closed doors. Rapper wasn't sure if it was because his injuries were so bad, or if it was because he was a known gang leader. Either way, the boys had been told right away that they wouldn't be seeing him anymore, so long as the hospital had anything to do with it. Under his breath, Rapper said a prayer for him. At least he would be all right...sooner or later.

Newbie's warm, white-tiled room felt like a safe haven—cut off from the outside world, cut off from the undercity. The rising sun shone through a picture window, creating an array of purples, magentas and soft pinks.

Rapper's shoe soles shuffled against the hard floor as he approached the hospital bed. Newbie was perfectly tucked inside the sheets. Off to the side, a heart monitor bleeped steadily with a bright, bouncing, lime-green line.

Newbie's left eye was surrounded by sunken black and blue impressions. His mouth was cut. His body was mostly hidden beneath the covers, but Rapper knew he was hurting. Rapper let out a long breath. He touched the boy's shoulder and Newbie's eyes fluttered open slowly.

"Hey, Rapper," he said, forcing out a smile. "Where're the others?"

"They only allowed one of us in here at a time," he explained. "Guess they think we're not to be trusted together."

"Where did they get that idea?"

Rapper wanted to smile at Newbie's little joke, but he couldn't bring himself to do it. The truth hurt.

"So, uh," Rapper stammered, "you still wanna be a Viper?"

Newbie squeezed his eyes closed tight for a second and then admitted, "It's not as fun as I thought it'd be."

"No, it's not."

A long, silent moment filled the room. Newbie reached up painfully and rolled his fingers over the tattoo on his neck.

"It's still there," Rapper reported.

"It'll be there forever, won't it?"

Rapper nodded. He wanted so badly to tell the boy that when his eyes and mouth and arm healed, the tattoo mark would disappear, too. But that would be a lie.

"I'll always be a part of the Vipers now," Newbie whispered. "You heard Strike First."

Rapper turned the back of his neck toward Newbie and pulled on his skin. He leaned down so Newbie could see. "See this?"

Newbie nodded as he studied the long scar.

"This," continued Rapper, "is from my Viper tattoo. I thought a little laser surgery would remove it. But guess what? This scar is almost worse. I can't see it very well, but I can *feel* it. And it's a constant reminder of my days with the Vipers."

"You trying to depress me?"

"No," Rapper said, standing back up, "I just want you to know something: That tattoo you have and the memories you got today...they may not go away so easily. But *you* can change."

Newbie sighed. "I dunno, Rapper. I know things are tough with the Vipers, but things aren't easy at home either. My mom and dad got divorced. My sister...I don't even know *what* she's doing anymore. I can't get good grades at school. Rad, it's just easier roughing with the Vipers."

"Easier, huh?" Rapper challenged. "You're 9 years old. If you continue with the Vipers, you may never make it to your thirteenth birthday. And you know how you'll be remembered? As a 30-second snippet on the evening news."

"But you heard what Strike First said. I can't get out! They won't let me go."

Rapper's forehead wrinkled. Newbie knew how it worked. It wasn't easy to get out. The Vipers wouldn't be pleased with "betrayal."

"I got out," Rapper said.

Newbie twisted his cut lip. "You don't look out to me."

"I'm just here temporarily. I'm a Superkid."

The surprise on Newbie's face was evident. "A *Superkid?!"*

"Yeah. My mom contacted Superkid Academy and that's how I got out. They helped me. Commander Kellie— she's the leader of my squad—made a way for me to enroll in the Academy and get away from the Vipers."

"But Superkid Academy may not be able to get me out—I've heard they're in a secret location now."

Rapper nodded. "There are places that can help you, Newbie. But you have to take the first step. Start by going to the police. You or someone you trust has to contact them. They know who to contact to help get you out and away—safe and sound."

Newbie stayed quiet and bit the inside of his lip. Rapper was ready to share the Word with him. He looked like he was ready to receive. Perhaps this situation would turn around for the better for Newbie.

"Hey, Newbie, I—"

BAM!

The hospital-room door slid open with force as a tall, dark-skinned man with short hair and a business suit entered. He was thin, but solid, and Rapper could tell by the sneer and the deep-set glare that he meant business.

"Get out of my son's room, gang-wrangler!" he cried, moving toward Rapper. The Superkid glanced back at Newbie who was nervously shaking his head. The heart-beat monitor bleeped faster.

Rapper put up his arms in surrender. The man kept moving toward him. Rapper knew he had to get out of there—*fast.* He couldn't blame Newbie's dad. His son was badly hurt. He was prepared to take revenge on the first gang member he saw. And Rapper, dressed in the Viper threads, passed for one.

Rapper kicked his feet forward and darted out of the room, barely missing Newbie's dad's thick arm. He ran

down the hall toward the waiting room, looking back periodically, expecting to see himself followed...but the angry
man never came. The Superkid slowed his pace and tried
to relax. This was a nightmare. He had to get away. He
had to contact Superkid Academy. He wanted to help
Jaws get out, too, but he knew he could help him better
with Commander Kellie and the other Superkids. If only
Strike First, Squealer and Jaws weren't in the waiting
room ahead, things would be so much easier.

Rapper entered the waiting room.

It was empty, save a little Asian lady knitting a pair
of pink booties. Rapper looked around. Magazines were
strewn about a coffee table. The television was spouting
the latest biased news on NME-TV. The snack machine
was out of item number C16, whatever that was. The
couches and the chairs were empty. Rapper wasn't sure
where the Vipers were, but suddenly he didn't really care.
This was his opportunity to contact Superkid Academy.

Suddenly his heart felt a longing he hadn't taken time
to allow himself to acknowledge. He thought of his friends,
who were certainly concerned for him and, no doubt, praying
'round the clock. He thought of Commander Kellie, the
Blue Squad's leader—he missed having her help and direction...and her friendship. He missed his roommates, Paul

and Alex, too. He imagined they were working double time
to try and find him. The two girls in the Blue Squad also
came to his mind. Missy, sassy and stubborn, was probably
praying for him at this very moment. And Valerie, a loyal
friend and a great pilot, was surely doing all she could do
as well.

What he would do to see them all now...

There were no signs indicating a ComPhone anywhere,
so he bolted down a hall opposite Newbie's room. His athletic shoes slapped the floor noisily.

Rapper slowed down to a jog when he turned the corner.
The hallway was jammed with six gurneys, four patients
and three medics. Rapper weaved in and out carefully,
trying not to bump any of the floating cots.

"Watch where you're going!" a doctor called Rapper's way.

"Where's a ComPhone?" Rapper asked, scooting along.

A nurse answered his question. "Take a right at the next
corner. It's across from the bathrooms. You all right, son?"

Rapper nodded courteously, but didn't slow down. He
rounded the corner as the nurse had instructed and saw the
ComPhone. The white box with video screen was only
40 feet away. Rapper glanced around for the Vipers, but
was relieved that he didn't see them anywhere. He glanced
at a digital clock midway down the hall. He had been away

from the room for only a minute...if he could get back in time, they'd never know.

Rapper punched in Superkid Academy's secret emergency number and hit the "call" button. The ComPhone video screen flashed white and a prerecorded female operator's face filled the screen. "We're sorry. We are unable to connect to the number you have dialed. Please recheck your number and—" Rapper hit the "Disconnect" button and the screen went blank. His hands were shaking from adrenaline. He was so nervous, he had dialed the wrong number. *Ugh!*

After dialing the number again, the screen flashed white and Commander Dana's face filled the video screen. Rapper's heart leapt.

"Rapper?!" the control room commander questioned. He leaned into his ComPhone's video screen.

Rapper opened his mouth to speak when—

"Hey!"

Rapper swallowed his words and turned his head when he heard the shout. It was a metallic voice—Jaws. Rapper whirled around and pressed his back against the ComPhone. His shoulder blade hit the "Disconnect" button and the screen went black.

Jaws meandered over and Rapper's mouth felt like cotton. What had he seen?

"Wha-what's up, rad?" Rapper asked, extending the Vipers' hand signal as a wave of greeting. His pinky shook as he tried to wiggle it like a snake's tongue.

Jaws' green eyes looked concerned as he angled his thumb to the bathroom. "Strike First and Squealer are in—"

The bathroom door slid open and the two Vipers came out laughing. Suddenly Strike First stopped.

"Rad, what are you doing here? You're supposed to be in with Newbie. What? You tryin' to sneak outta here without us knowin'?" Strike First clenched his fist.

Squealer narrowed his eyes accusingly.

Strike First slapped one hand into another. "Perhaps you need some help remembering who your family is," he threatened.

Rapper braced himself, but wouldn't let his gaze fall. "I know exactly who my family is," he retorted.

"Do you?" Strike First took a step forward. He glanced over to Jaws and asked, "Jaws, is our rad here telling the truth? You were out here—you should know."

Jaws looked at Rapper and back to Strike First and then at Squealer. His cheeks flushed above his leather-and-steel jaw brace. His green eyes returned to search Rapper's.

"He's telling the truth," Jaws replied after what seemed like an eternity. "I saw him. He didn't do anything unusual."

Rapper blinked noticeably as he felt the tension leave his body. He wasn't sure what Jaws had seen…but if he had seen anything, he wasn't telling.

A security guard making his rounds appeared at the far end of the hall.

"Hey, c'mon, rad," Squealer said, tapping Strike First on the back. "Rapper was probably just lookin' for us. Let's get outta here."

Strike First released his tightened fist. "All right," he said to Squealer. Then to Rapper: "But I'll be watching *you* closely."

"Give me a break," Rapper said, tired and irritable.

"I already gave you a break, rad!"

Rapper didn't like it. He hadn't asked to be here and now every move he tried to make was being controlled. He needed a break...but Strike First was the last one who wanted to give it to him.

It was early afternoon and Rapper already found himself wanting to be back at the hospital. He would even be willing to face Newbie's dad again—anything to get out of the undercity. He felt like the concrete walls were closing in. With no windows anywhere, it was easy to lose track of time. You never knew whether it was sunny or cloudy, rainy or windy, day or night. Yes, Rapper needed a break...a good *long* one from the Vipers.

But the more he thought about getting out, the more his spirit yearned to see the victims of the undercity set free. He felt for kids like Newbie and Jaws...and even Strike First and Squealer. Sure, they had made their own choices—but they had also been influenced by their environment, blinded by Satan. How else could a kid possibly believe life in the undercity was decent?

Rapper thought about all the reasons someone might join a gang: identity, recognition, belonging, discipline, hope for love, greed for money. He wondered just what had lured Strike First and Squealer. He wondered what had enticed Newbie and Jaws. He thought about what had pulled him in years ago. Now that he was a Christian, he was able to look back on that old life and see how Satan had done his work.

Rapper had joined the Vipers back then in hopes of finding somewhere to belong...hoping for love...searching for identity. But contrary to what had been promised, none of those things had been found in the undercity gang. Sure, at times, he felt like he belonged and was respected. But take his laser-slicer away and who respected him then? The respect he had was borne out of fear...fear of what he might have done to someone if they *didn't* respect him.

Rapper wondered if maybe this was all part of a plan carefully woven by God. Was there someone here Rapper needed to share the Word with? Strike First? Squealer? Jaws? Newbie? Did God have a purpose in all this? Or was this just Satan's trap and Rapper needed only to get free? And if so, how would *he* do that? Suddenly Rapper realized he'd been thinking a whole lot about numero uno. He thought *he* could keep his promise and rescue Python. He thought *he* could protect Newbie. He thought *he* could escape.

Rapper snapped back to the present as he became aware of Strike First's lanky body pacing the floor of the Vipers' Common Room. He looked fresh again, his fiery-red hair combed back. Rapper leaned against a painted, cartoon-snake's rattle on a rough wall.

"I'm just asking you to cut me some slack," Rapper said simply.

"Oh, now our rad's asking for a favor," Strike First blurted out.

Squealer stepped in the room with Jaws close behind him. Both the boys looked refreshed. Their hair was also neatly combed; Jaws' shoulder-length, white hair was slickly pulled back in his ponytail. Both, like Strike First and Rapper, still wore their Viper gear.

"The guys are snoozin'," Squealer reported nonchalantly. He sat down in a rolling chair and scooted across the concrete to a computer terminal. Jaws stood beside the desk, periodically checking a connection or two on the back of the computer.

"Ain't you tired?" Strike First asked Jaws with a nod

of his head. Jaws scratched the back of his head.

"No," he responded, his voice reverberating.

"You look tired," Strike First observed, letting it drop. Rapper had to agree. The boy's eyes were red and his cheeks looked pale. Rapper wondered if he had been crying. Of course, he didn't ask. No Viper or Viper-in-training would ever admit to any kind of emotion— especially one that involved tears.

"What's up with you?" Squealer casually asked Strike First.

"What's up with *me?*" Strike First spat back, his spindly form moving across the room. *"Rapper* is what's up with me. Our mission was ruined last night because we followed his plan. We lost members."

"Whoa-whoa," Rapper interrupted Strike First's discourse. "Let's get some things straight here. I didn't ask to be here. C'mon. Years ago, I was made the 'sipe. I agreed to help out since I had given my word in blood. Innocent kids were hurt—but not because of me. I was trying to run a safe mission." Rapper pointed straight at Strike First as adrenaline mixed with his anger. "They were hurt because this is the undercity. You don't see it, but this is no way to live! This isn't the way things should happen. Kids shouldn't be risking their lives! Newbie should be in school—not getting beaten up by a 13-year-old thug. Newbie...Newbie shouldn't be recruited as some kind of *buffer!*"

Rapper nodded toward Jaws fervently. "A *buffer*—Jaws. Did you know that's why you were recruited? They don't care about you! They brought you here to take a beating so someone else—someone who's bigger and older—wouldn't have to!"

Jaws looked down. He rubbed his finger on a strip of metal on his jaw brace. Squealer was looking down too. He had stopped computing for a moment. Strike First was frowning and glaring at Rapper.

"I'm sorry," Rapper shouted, waving his right arm through the air, "but it's the truth! Nobody here really cares about anyone else—everyone's out to save their own rep. Reputation, that's what it's all about. That and revenge. But it's sin—plain and simple. And it leads to death in the end."

"You don't know nothin' about the undercity!" Strike First challenged. "We're here 'cuz we need each other! We are here 'cuz we need family!"

"No!" Rapper shouted back, marching toward Strike First with his finger straight out. "This place is *nothing* about family. This place nearly robbed three families of their sons last night!"

"You don't know nothin' about those guys! How do

you know they had families?!"

"Because my brother had a family!" Rapper choked on his words, and could barely find his voice to continue. "My brother was killed by the undercity," he explained, much softer. "He thought he was looking for family, too. But he already had one. And he was stolen from it. Don't tell me I don't know about the undercity. I know all about it. I know it steals, kills and destroys, just like the devil who runs it. And may God have mercy on the ones like you who are blinded...and the ones like the kid who killed my brother...who are on the path to destruction."

Strike First stomped over to a steel desk across the room. He pulled open the top drawer, pulled out an item and held it in front of him. Rapper felt his knees go weak when he realized what it was—the Electroblade. Strike First tightened his grip around the weapon and it lit up, flashing electric light around the room.

Jaws became wide-eyed and scooted to the side. Squealer looked puzzled.

"Wha-where'd you get that?" Squealer asked.

"This—*this* is the future of the Vipers," Strike First stated, his thin lips curling. He looked at Rapper. "You wanna know about destruction? Let me tell you 'bout destruction. *This* is the weapon that will save the undercity. This is the weapon that will stop the killing. You want family? You want respect? Well, so do I! And this weapon will give it to us! The undercity will stand in fear of the gang that has this weapon. And now it's ours. We have the only one. And we can and will make more."

"But I thought Python had that," Rapper eyed Strike First.

"Now I have it. What of it?"

"Python's chest...it had a burn on it. I thought it was from—"

"Python couldn't lead the undercity to peace. He didn't see what I see!"

"I don't believe you—"

"I am the leader of the Vipers now!"

"You?!" Rapper disbelieved. "I thought I was the 'sipe!"

"Python's out of the picture," Strike First stated. "If he ever gets better, he'll be locked up. He won't be back any time soon."

On the side, Squealer cracked a smile.

"So," Strike First continued, "he's as good as dead to us. That means your 'sipe duties are over. I'm in charge now." Strike First smiled wickedly.

Rapper felt weak. Strike First was the self-proclaimed, new Vipers' leader. His wishes would become the gang's command. What would this mean for the undercity? What would it mean to the world above?

The computer warbled and Squealer gave it his sudden attention. Strike First and Rapper didn't take their eyes off each other.

"Rad!" Squealer shouted. "Check it!"

Strike First walked over to the computer authoritatively. Rapper felt a sinking feeling in his stomach.

"What?" Strike First asked.

"I was running the daily scan," Squealer responded. "Check it. A few hours ago, some kind of encrypted message was sent out of here. I can't read it, but I *can* tell that it was supposed to be a secret. There're all kinds of frequency codes sent around it to disguise it."

Strike First turned to Rapper. "Well, well. *Someone* didn't realize our systems were as chill as they thought. I guess Superkid Academy is a bit behind the times, huh?"

Rapper's mouth went dry. "Hey—whoa. I didn't send out any message."

"Where were you—" Strike First glanced at the screen, "—exactly 78 minutes ago?"

"Walking around the caverns," Rapper said. He wanted to add, *trying to find a way out,* but didn't.

Strike First held the stick-like weapon in front of Rapper's face. Rapper could feel the heat from the electricity smack his skin.

"You've been tryin' to get away from here since the moment you came," the Viper leader whispered threateningly. "I knew you were trying to dust us in the hospital. And now you send a secret message? Calling Superkid Academy, were you? I think you led us to the Claws without any weapons for a reason. You been tryin' to betray us from the start!"

The Electroblade went black and Strike First whirled around. He punched a few buttons on his watch and then threw the weapon back into the drawer. It slammed against the back and the drawer shut fast with the force of the throw.

"Never forget, traitor, that Strike First is the leader of the Vipers. You *will* respect me."

* * *

Bruised and exhausted, Rapper lay alone at the bottom of a large, empty pit. A swooshing sound came from above him, but he was too tired to move. He had been beaten without mercy…it was the way the underground dealt with troublemakers. Every muscle ached. Every appendage throbbed. He had gotten what Strike First thought he deserved…even if he didn't deserve it. He kept his burning eyes shut.

The swooshing stopped. He heard a thump. He knew someone was behind him. He could hear clothes brush together as the person moved. A pinch on Rapper's left shoulder was followed by a hiss. He began to jerk away, but a firm hand caught him. "It's medicine; it'll help," a soft voice whispered in his left ear. He relaxed and took in the musty scent of the rock he was lying on. He had no strength left to do anything except trust the stranger.

A warm hand touched his forehead for a long moment. A heartbeat passed. Then another. And another.

The soft voice spoke again. It said, "This is the word of the Lord to you:

"All rising tongues shall fall as a drop of life descends.
The right Weapon changes what was to what will be.
Wield It well and find your future where your history
begins, Where vices are transformed into debris."

The hand lifted from his forehead. Rapper heard the mysterious helper arise and steadily climb away.

Rapper's eyes burned as he tried to focus. The sticky air seemed to layer upon him as he sat up. The big pit was empty. Brick surrounded him and cement lay under him. A small, dark hole far above him was the only way in or out. From it was draped a long, black rope, daring him to escape. He didn't have the strength.

With a little difficulty, Rapper slid himself over to the wall under the hole. He pushed himself into a seated position and leaned back, though it wasn't as comfortable as he had hoped.

The throbbing in his head made focusing difficult. His back ached with knots. His neck cramped. His legs felt like jelly. Rapper's brother died as a result of another gang's violence. A fleeting thought made Rapper wonder if he would be a victim, too...only his *own* gang would be responsible.

No, that wasn't right. It wasn't his gang. He wanted no part of it. They may be forcing him to stay. They may be keeping him from outside contact. But they would never be able to make him part of a gang again.

He wondered how his face looked. His body was bruised in about 30 places—he could feel it. He hardly remembered what had happened. One moment, he was talking with Strike First, the next moment there was a fist in his face.

Rapper wondered what time it was. Somewhere in the dark room a rat scampered along the floor, its claws clicking. It wasn't exactly paradise... Rapper thought back to his recent vacation on Calypso Island with Valerie's family, the Riveras. All the Superkids were supposed to go, but circumstances at the last minute changed their plans. Rapper and Valerie were the only two who ended up on the island (though finally getting them both there had been quite an adventure).

Rapper closed his eyes and dreamed of that golden Calypso Island sun, its beams spilling over his shoulders. Swimming in the ocean, eating roasted boar. Rapper's mouth began to water. Good friends, good food, good fun—Rapper had no idea that just a short time later he would be minus all three, in a Vipers' dungeon.

Reeling in his thoughts, Rapper prayed, "Remember your word to your servant, for you have given me hope," Psalm 119:49. Strength trickled in as his hope arose. This was part of what it was to be a Superkid. Sure, troubles may come...no, troubles *would* come. But when they came, a Superkid had hope. "My comfort in my suffering is this: Your promise preserves my life. The arrogant mock me without restraint, but I do not turn from your law. I remember your ancient laws, O Lord, and I find comfort in them" (verses 50-52).

Hope stirred inside Rapper as he prayed...and the previous night's mysterious prophecy reentered his mind. Had that really happened? *Yes,* he thought. *It did.* Who was that? An angel?

A beaming, yellow light in the room above came on and shot down the hole, illuminating the grime.

"Hey there, rad! Look at our little rebel now!"

The voice was distinct, taunting. Strike First's skinny framework crept over the hole above, casting an eerie, long shadow into the cavern below.

"I need something to eat," Rapper managed to say. He wasn't about to beg, but he was hungry.

Strike First nodded to the side. "Been comfy, rad?" he asked.

Rapper pushed himself into a straighter seated position. He looked up at his captor. "Well, it's not exactly paradise."

Strike First had come for a reason. "Somebody called last night," he began.

Rapper wasn't interested. "How long are you going to leave me down here?"

"Nobody's stoppin' you. You can use the rope and come up when you're ready."

Rapper eyed the rope.

"I said somebody called."

He was holding the bait. Rapper decided to go ahead and bite. "Who?" he asked.

"The Claws," Strike First said with a wicked smile. "They're tired of fighting. Guess they know we're more powerful now that we've got the Electroblade tech. They're toast."

"Good," Rapper said flatly. "The fighting has to stop somewhere."

"I'm glad you feel like that."

"What do I have to do with it?" Rapper wondered.

Strike First sat down on the edge of the opening. He let his long legs dangle down. He picked up the rope and began to wind it up around his wrist.

"Everything, rad...*everything.*"

Rapper felt the pressure of the words. He didn't know what they meant, but he was sure it wasn't good. He waited for Strike First to continue.

"The Claws have challenged us."

"What kind of challenge?"

"A fight."

"Naturally," Rapper said, disappointed.

Strike First clicked his heels against the side of the cavern. The sound echoed.

"But this fight'll be different. It won't be our whole gang against theirs. They have one bad rad—and they want him to fight against one of us. They say whoever wins, that gang gets the others' complete territory and tech."

Rapper suddenly saw where this was leading. "You want me to be your David against their Goliath." He said it more as a statement than a question.

"He's a genius!" Strike First shouted. "Let's face it—no one here wants to stop the fighting more than you. Here's your chance. Besides, we found out you weren't the rad sending out secret messages. Squealer found another one was sent last night. And you were too beaten to send it."

"So who sent it?"

Strike First's thin lips curled. "Don't know. We'll find 'em." Rapper knew better than to say anything, but he wondered if there was a connection between his midnight visitor and the one who sent out the message.

As Rapper sat still for a moment, considering Strike First's words, he thought of his brother. *Nicholas shouldn't have had to die.* What if there was a way to stop the fighting? What if Rapper won the fight and put the Claws out of commission? Sure, there were other gangs around—meaner gangs, even. But he would be able to stop two from fighting.

No, that's not right, he reasoned. *What good does it do to stop fighting by fighting?* He didn't want any part of it. Not as a Superkid. Not as Rapper.

"Well, I'm not in any condition to fight," he said.

"I had to be sure you weren't our traitor, rad. But now I know the truth. That's why I had your mark of loyalty reapplied. It'll be on forever now."

Rapper touched the back of his neck. He felt his scar...but his skin also felt tender. He thought it was just from the beating. Rapper swallowed hard as his stomach felt queasy.

"Here," Strike First said, dropping down a compact mirror. Rapper caught the thin square in midair. Carefully, he held it up to the light and angled his head sideways. As he peered into the mirror, he saw some shades of green peeking out from around his neck. His stomach muscles tightened.

Rapper tapped a small up-arrow on the glass and the mirror zoomed in on his neck. The green color

magnified to show a scaly pattern. Rapper threw the
mirror on the ground, cracking it. Up above, Strike
First let out a roaring laugh.

"You had *no right* to do this!" Rapper shouted, looking
up, longing to climb the rope and let Strike First have it.
"I'm *not* a Viper any longer!"

"You look like one to me, rad."

"I've *changed!*" Rapper cried.

"Who are you trying to convince?" Strike First countered. "Me or you?"

"I'm *not* fighting anyone! The Superkid manual says I
don't fight against flesh and blood."

Strike First chuckled again. "We'll see. When you're
standing in the center of the ring and Goliath is coming at
you, you'll have to do something. You'll fight."

"I won't fight."

"You *will* fight. By the way, it's a fight to the death."

"Oh, now I get it. If I win, great. The Vipers rule the
undercity. And if I lose, that's fine, too. You won't stop the
fighting and you won't have lost anyone important to you.
In other words, I'm just a *buffer.*"

Squealer appeared above and tossed down a few
apples, two cans of soda and a banana. Strike First let the
rope drop down into the room again.

"Well, rad, the rope ain't movin'. Come out when you're ready. The fight is tomorrow night, so you have till then," Strike First offered. "You best get up as quickly as you can. The food's better up here and there are more comfortable places to rest."

Rapper looked at the rope and felt his strength wane. He would be staying a little longer.

Three apples and a banana were enough to give
Rapper the energy he needed to make the short trek up
the rope. A sip of the soda was what gave him the moti-
vation—to find something heartier.

Every step Rapper took toward the main cavern was
punctuated with a healing scripture.

First Peter 2:24 says that, "by His wounds I have
been healed," Rapper said.

"Your Word is life to me and health to my whole
body—Proverbs 4:22."

"Jesus came that I may have life, and have it to the
full—John 10:10."

The Word working in him was already building his
strength. Rapper entered the main cavern and chose to
ignore the curious stares of the Vipers. He heard a
Serfsled or two zip by overhead and ignored them, too.
He stumbled to the kitchen, which was nothing more
than another hole in the cavern, grabbed some bottled
fruit juice and rested upon a graffiti-laden rock.

Grabbing a handful of pretzels, Rapper tried to

remember the last time he had a well-rounded meal. The Vipers didn't seem to care too much about nutrition despite the fruit they had on hand. They ate fruit because it was cheap and tasty—not because it was good for them. If fruit was expensive and *Frosted Wheatsie Eatsies* cereal was available at a rock-bottom price, then the cereal would suddenly become their mainstay.

The juice stung a bit going down his throat, like a spice hidden in a cool salsa. Nonetheless, he welcomed the meal. His energy had returned and Rapper was pleased at how well he was feeling. Being in the light, he was able to confirm what he had suspected: he had more than one bruise on his body, but nothing was sprained, cut or broken.

Rapper had been resting for about an hour, moving little, when Jaws entered the room. Like a squirrel, he froze when he spied Rapper in the corner. He looked as though he were about to turn and run when Rapper spoke up.

"Surprised to see me back so soon?" he asked before popping another handful of pretzels in his mouth.

"Not really," Jaws said relaxing. He looked behind himself before coming farther into the kitchen.

"Don't worry," Rapper comforted. "They won't care if they see you with me. It's me they're wanting to put the pressure on, not you."

"Can I ask you something?" Jaws asked. His computer voice actuator echoed in the room. He didn't bother to sit. Rapper nodded. "You said earlier that they let me become a Viper so I could be a buffer. Is that true?"

"What do you think?" Rapper challenged.

Jaws' face fell. "They do that with a lot of kids?" he asked.

Rapper nodded.

"They do that with Newbie?"

Rapper nodded again. "Now can I ask you a question?"

Jaws nodded.

"Why did you help me out in the hospital? You knew I was calling Superkid Academy, yet you didn't tell Strike First and Squealer."

Jaws shrugged his shoulders. His cheekbones rose as he admitted, "There's something different about you."

Rapper smiled weakly, raised his eyebrows and touched the back of his neck. "Sometimes I wonder," he said, sighing.

Jaws looked at Rapper eye-to-eye. His green eyes were set as he said, "Don't." Then he turned and exited the room.

* * *

That one word from Jaws hit Rapper right in the chest. "Don't." Just "don't." *Don't* begin to wonder if you are the same as you were before. *Don't* even go there. That word came from someone who most surely didn't even know the Lord, but it hit him with the force of a sailing baseball.

Rapper knew God's Word. He knew it said in 2 Corinthians 5:17 that he was a new creation—all old things had gone and everything had become new. He knew he shouldn't look back at his old life. He knew he should press on toward the goal to win the prize for which God had called him, like Philippians 3:14 said. That's what he *should* do.

So he took a long, spirit-building walk around the Vipers' hideout and over the catwalks. Praying in the spirit encouraged him. He let the Holy Spirit direct his prayer because he didn't know exactly what to pray himself. By the time he wandered into the Vipers' Common Room Rapper was feeling much stronger and more confident.

He found Squealer sitting hunched over a computer on the far side of the room and Strike First was at his side. They were both staring at the monitor as Squealer punched a control panel and white numbers on a blue background scrolled down the screen.

"Still haven't found your secret message sender?" Rapper prodded.

Strike First turned around and smiled. "Welcome

back, rad."

"Twenty-four hours ago you weren't so happy to see me," Rapper countered. Strike First frowned.

"You keep dissin' me," he scolded. "That's what got you in trouble in the first place."

Rapper decided not to send the ball back into his court. "Just dropped by to tell you once again that I'm not fighting. Go ahead and beat me. It'll just ensure your loss."

"That's the way I like you, rad—spittin' fire."

Strike First walked over to the desk the Electroblade was stored in and opened up the drawer. He pulled out the weapon and walked over to Rapper. He grabbed his hand and slapped the Electroblade into it.

Jaws entered at the edge of the room. He watched closely.

"You will be fighting, whether you go of your own free will or whether we have to drag you into the arena," Strike First promised. "Now I suggest you go out there with this weapon. Keep in mind that the Claw will be coming out with his own bag of tricks."

Rapper glanced over at Jaws, then looked down at the Electroblade. He rolled the weapon over in his hands and then walked back across the room. He carefully returned the weapon to the drawer.

"I'm not fighting," he replied. "You can force me to go

out there but I won't do it."

"You say that now," Strike First observed, "but tomorrow night, when the pressure's on, you're gonna want the juice. When you do"—Strike First nodded toward the drawer—"you'll know just where to get it."

Rapper shut the drawer.

* * *

Best Rapper could judge, there were only about 15 hours left until the fight. He couldn't sleep, so he began walking around again, praying and wondering what would come next. He wanted to just escape or to try sending a secret message of his own, but he couldn't think of any way to do it where he would actually still be alive at the end.

Turning a corner, Rapper froze. Drawn on a dark wall in a small, secluded hallway, Rapper saw a large, cartoon face of a young boy, 12 years old. He had a medium nose, blond hair and a "go get 'em" look. One eye was shut tight. His teeth were showing as he was smiling from the side of his mouth. Written across the bottom were the words:

GRRR!!!
6.18
HE HAD THE JUICE

AveNge!

Grrr. Rapper knew this Viper. Grrr's real name was Nicholas Rapfield—Rapper's brother. This was how the undercity remembered him. This was his token tombstone—a mere scrawling on a darkened, out-of-the-way wall. Rapper closed his eyes.

"God, I believe I'm new on the inside like Your Word says," he prayed, "but I don't feel very new right now. I've got this identity branded on my neck, but it's not me anymore. Holy Spirit, show me if there's anything in my life that might keep Your power from flowing through me.

"I want...no, I *need* to experience Your power in my life every day. I'm dead to this life with the Vipers. Father, I want to live out the life-giving power You've placed in me. Remind me who I am in You. Remind me who You called me to be. In Jesus' Name, amen."

He had the juice—avenge! Rapper touched the word "avenge." Briefly, he wondered what his memorial would say. Maybe "He didn't belong here," or even "He stopped the fighting." Maybe it would be a rap: "He stood for right/he wouldn't fight."

In the end, to Rapper it didn't matter. But one thing he knew for sure: There wouldn't be an "avenge" written under his name. No one would avenge him. He was their David...but also their buffer. To the Vipers, if he didn't serve their purposes every day, his life didn't matter. He silently wished he had known that truth many years ago before he had ever joined in the first place.

Rapper didn't have a Bible with him, so he continued to rely upon the Word he had put in his heart. He spoke it to himself and prayed...and prayed...and prayed. He knew he wanted to live his new life, but among the Vipers, he wasn't sure how.

Rapper rubbed his palms over his eyes and yawned. He was tired, but too tired to sleep. Slowly, he walked back into the main coliseum and rested against a wall. The high catwalks had occasional activity. A young boy running from one cave to another. Some talking. None laughing. Perhaps they, too, realized their future was in Rapper's hands...and he was determined not to fight for it. Not if it meant bloodshed. It just wasn't right. A Serfsled zipped by above, its clear base casting a wide, light shadow over the ground.

Rapper knew this was where he would be forced to fight...or at least forced to be beaten in front of two gangs. The concrete was hard and made his legs feel heavy. He sighed deeply.

Crossing the room, Rapper made his way to a long, black, steel stairway leading to the first level of catwalks. He strode across, praying and thinking. Rapper ran his fingers along the cool, metal railing. How he longed, as the minutes rolled by, to be back at Superkid Academy—to have life be normal again. But something told Rapper that within the next 15 hours or so, his life was sure to change forever. Once he was forced into that ring, he would have to be ready to give his life if he had to. He wouldn't fight. He wouldn't be a bad example to the other Vipers and the Claws. He was a Superkid. And he didn't fight with flesh and blood. He had made up his mind. Again.

Rapper was jolted back to matters at hand when he heard an echo in the cavern. A shriek. Not a shriek of happiness or even fright...but a cry of...surprise.

Looking around the room from his perch, Rapper couldn't figure out what direction the cry had come from.

"No!!!"

There it was again—from below. Rapper took off down the catwalk and rode the railing down the stairway. At the bottom, he hopped off and looked around. He saw a flicker of light from the tunnel leading to the Vipers' Common Room. With energy like a cheetah chasing down its prey, Rapper sprinted to the Commons.

He froze at the doorway. Strike First was approaching someone. His fist was in the air. He reached forward and grabbed the boy's shoulder.

Rapper mouthed the boy's name in surprise. What could he have possibly done?

"Your spying days are over!" Strike First spat at him. He grabbed the back of Jaws' neck and yanked at his jaw brace. The leather and metal contraption snapped away and dropped to the ground. Rapper gasped when he saw Jaws' face without the brace.

There were no scars or tears. No surgical implants or stitches. His face was perfect. Only seconds went by, but the longer Rapper stared at the face, the more he realized he recognized it. Without the mask, without the cheeks pulled back like stretched cloth, without the voice activator to change his voice...it looked just like...it sounded just like...

Strike First gasped, too, and pulled back his fist in anger. He threw his punch, passionate to make contact. The spy screamed once again and Rapper ran forward. As the fist headed toward the spy's face, Rapper grabbed Strike First's arm in motion and stopped it cold. Caught off guard, Strike First reeled back and lost his balance. The Viper leader hit the ground backward, smashing against it with his back-end and his pride.

Rapper's face softened as he took in the intruder. He could hardly believe it.

"I can't believe you bleached your hair," he said with a weak smile. "Thanks for keeping an eye on me."

"Getting caught wasn't part of the plan," the spy said sheepishly. "I'm sorry."

"Don't be," Rapper replied, shaking his head. He helped the young spy out of the corner. "Strike First," he addressed, looking down at the fallen leader, "I'd like you to meet a friend of mine, a very good friend, Valerie Rivera."

Strike First pushed himself up and tapped his watch.

"I caught your 'friend' trying to send out another message," he uttered menacingly. "She'll get what she deserves for messing with us."

"No one messes with Valerie," Rapper stated strongly, taking a stand between Strike First and the Superkid.

"You seem to feel very strongly about that."

"Stronger than you want to know."

A small garrison of Vipers arrived at the entrance and Strike First motioned them toward Valerie. Rapper eyed them warily and tightened his fists.

"No one hurts her," Strike First ordered to Rapper's

surprise. "Just throw her in cell 2-B."

The Vipers looked at Rapper, not wanting to approach until he let down his guard. Rapper turned to Valerie. "It'll be all right," he promised.

"Hey," she responded with a smile, "I know."

Rapper squeezed her shoulder. It was so good to see a familiar face. Suddenly the midnight helper who had visited him and given him the prophecy made perfect sense.

One of the Vipers stepped forward and took hold of Valerie's arm. Rapper nodded to her and she nodded back. Rapper let go and the Vipers led Valerie out of the room.

* * *

"How are you doing?" Rapper asked. The room was dimly lit in yellow like so many of the Vipers' caves. This one seemed especially dark though, since it held one of Rapper's good friends captive. The Vipers hadn't bothered to station a guard in front of Valerie's cell—their experience told them the bars were sturdy enough and the walls were thick enough to prevent anyone from escaping. Each wall, decorated with slithering, cartoonish snakes, reminded the Superkids where they were.

Valerie was still in her Vipers' uniform—the dark, denim shorts; the lightweight, dark-brown jacket; the olive T-shirt; the black athletic shoes. She stood, leaning into the front of the cage. Her arms pressed against the bars on one side, Rapper's pressed against the bars on the other.

Valerie grimaced. "How am *I* doing?" she asked. "I should be asking you that question."

"Why? You're the one behind bars."

"I've been here as long as you have, Rapper. I know what's coming. Don't forget what's happening tonight."

Rapper tried to change the subject. "I still can't believe you bleached your hair. And you're wearing those silly contacts. I should have known that wasn't your real eye color. They're green—like a lime."

Valerie cupped her left hand under her right eye and used the other to slide her contact down and out. She repeated the process with her left eye. Squeezing her eyelids tight, she tossed the colored contacts to the floor.

"Wow. It feels good to get rid of those. Like taking off your shoes at night."

"It's been awhile since I've taken off my shoes."

"I know."

The room dropped silent for a moment. Valerie looked at Rapper with her real, soft-brown eyes. "Hey, it's gonna be all right. God will get us through this."

Rapper scratched at the pavement with his shoe. "Do you think it was right for me to lead the others into the

Claws' den?"

"Rapper, what's past is past. You did what you thought was right at the time. What you have to do now is go to the Lord about tonight. The fight is only hours away."

"I should have gone to the Lord from the beginning. Ugh! I've been making all these decisions on my own. What's gotten into me? Since when did I fall back into being the kind of person I was...always thinking *I* can do it—me and me alone?"

"Rapper—"

"No!" Rapper interrupted, pushing away from the bars. Then he caught himself. "I'm sorry. It's just...Newbie's condition is *my* fault. All because I thought I knew how to protect him best."

"Rapper, what if you hadn't been there? It could have been much worse."

Rapper hit his fist against a snake's face on the cement wall. It hurt more than it helped. "Now *you're* in a cell, I've got a death sentence, Strike First is leading the Vipers to certain trouble..."

"Rapper, if it wasn't for you, I might not be alive. And don't forget who you are. You're Rapper—a godly young man who was willing to give up his life to save a friend."

Rapper looked at Valerie, sadly. He leaned back in

against the bars, taking a stand beside his friend. He had known Valerie as long as he had known any of the other Superkids—for four years. And for a girl, he thought, she wasn't half bad. Valerie and he were the two star pilots in the Academy, so they had spent a lot of time studying similar subjects together: engine analysis, technical systems and flight exams. There was something he had to let her know—it wouldn't be fair not to...

"I've changed my mind about the fight tomorrow night."

Valerie tipped her head. Rapper missed seeing her usually dark-brown hair bounce on her shoulders. Her lips parted in surprise.

"What do you mean?" she asked.

Rapper felt his throat tighten.

"I mean I've decided to fight the Claw."

"You mean like hand-to-hand combat?"

"As opposed to...?"

"Rapper, don't joke about this. Strike First said it's a fight to the death. You can't kill him."

"He'd kill *me.*"

"How do you know that?"

Rapper stayed silent.

"What?" Valerie prodded. "Rapper, listen to me. How do you think you'll feel if you fight him?"

"How will I feel if I don't?"

"Do you really want to put Strike First in charge of not just one, but *two* gangs?"

"No, I don't, but—"

"What?"

"It'll be self-defense. It's not like I *want* to do it."

"Self-defense? Rapper, the Lord is your strong Defender. He'll take up your case. Remember Proverbs 23:11, and don't worry about me. The Lord—"

"You don't understand," Rapper interrupted. "I wasn't there to save my brother, but I can't let that happen again!"

"What? You're making no sense."

Rapper paused. He didn't want to say it. He didn't want to apply the pressure. But it wasn't fair for her not to know.

"Strike First raised the stakes," Rapper admitted softly. "He said if I don't fight...the next memorial on the wall will be yours."

Valerie stood in stunned silence. Rapper pushed away from the bars once again.

"So," he continued in a whisper, "unless you have something up your sleeve...well...let's just hope I win. It's been awhile."

Valerie shook her head emphatically. "No...no...it's not...no! Rapper, listen, I've got—"

"Valerie!" Rapper threw up his hands. "You can't make me decide between you and some ruthless Claw. I lost my brother. I'm not going to lose you!"

"Rapper, that happened a long time ago! You can't let a past failure be more real to you than God's promise. Rapper, think of who you are now!" she shouted, gripping the bars. "Rapper!"

Rapper gritted his teeth and swiftly exited the cavern.

Echoing with cries and shouts, the Vipers' main coliseum was the focal point for the nearly 100 kids gathered. From ages 6 to 22, the Vipers and the Claws had no trouble coming up with threats and cursings to hurl at one another.

The Vipers were clearly separated from the Claws, taking their stand on the left side of the gigantic, cement auditorium. In this way, they protected their Commons, most of the catwalk stairs and all private room entrances. The Claws, just as distrustful, stood on the other side of the room, guarding any outlet that might lead to their empty quarters. And everyone was watching his back.

Rapper could feel his stomach churning as he peered across the crowd and wondered which Claw he was about to fight. Periodically, he glanced up at the catwalk 30 feet above. Valerie was up there, each wrist chained behind her to the cold steel railing. It wasn't much, but it was more than enough to keep her from escaping. Strike First had ordered for her to be displayed up there as a constant reminder to Rapper that he'd better give the fight everything within him.

Adrenaline zipped through Rapper like electricity

through a circuit board. Rapper knew he would be quite a match for any Claw with his Superkid defense training and the "street ways" he had learned long ago.

Strike First brushed by Rapper and slapped him on the back. "All right, rad," he congratulated. "I knew you wouldn't let me down!"

Rapper's eyes squinted as he wondered what Strike First meant. Squealer was close behind. "I knew you wouldn't leave it!"

"What?!" Rapper said, grabbing Squealer's sleeve.

"Sure, play dumb," Squealer said sarcastically, pulling himself away. He moved through the crowd of Vipers.

"What are you talking ab—"

SCREEEEEEEEECH!!!

Loudspeakers Rapper didn't even know were in the coarse walls jolted to life. Strike First, standing on a large rock, shouted into a cordless microphone hooked around his head.

"Today marks the end of our wars! This is history!" Strike First shouted. The Vipers hissed, the Claws growled. Rapper felt like moaning. "One rad from each of our camps will fight to the death...and the winning rad decides our fate...or our victory! Who will rule? The Claws?" Roars came from the Claws, boos from the Vipers. "Or...the

Vipers!!!" This time, the Vipers roared, trying their hardest to drown out the opposite side's disapproval.

Rapper suddenly found himself being lifted above the Vipers' heads as they all began chanting his name confidently.

"Rap-per! Rap-per! Rap-per!"

The group of kids pushed him forward and dropped him at the edge of the vast circle between the two contending gangs. Rapper stepped onto the edge of the large floor painting of the Vipers' snake symbol. Rapper noted how hard the ground still felt...it hadn't changed a bit since he had first arrived. He remembered when he was younger that he had gotten used to the rock-solid cement. He certainly wasn't used to it now.

The Vipers quieted down momentarily as the Claws shouted a name once, in unity.

"Slayer!"

Rapper winced. *Why did his name have to be "Slayer"?*

The Claws parted right down the middle of their group, making a clear pathway between the ring and a tunnel in the wall. From out of the tunnel, a shadow crawled across the floor, like the shadow of a cloud sliding in front of the sun.

The one called "Slayer" pressed his way out of the

tunnel somewhat awkwardly. His large frame barely fit. Rapper looked up as Slayer stood tall. Easily 6 feet tall, a clear head above the other Claws, Slayer's very presence commanded his respect.

Long, dark hair and a dark face were accented by his deep-set eyes and wide lips. Slayer was somewhere in his mid-to-late teens, Rapper guessed. His midnight-black clothes fit him tightly like a superhero's suit, allowing his muscles to bulge and intimidate the enemy. His arms were folded across his chest.

Though Rapper thought it was a bit dramatic, Slayer boldly wore a thin, coal-colored cape that rolled behind every step he took. Rapper's audible gulp was an understatement. When Slayer reached the ring's unmarked outside boundary, he unfolded his arms and revealed a thick glove that engulfed his right hand and part of his arm. As he clenched his fist, electricity zapped across his knuckles. This was surely ten times as powerful as the electric knuckle weapons Rapper had seen earlier. The Vipers gasped. Out of the corner of his eye, Rapper saw Strike First lower his head. Rapper glanced up at Valerie. She stood gaping, shaking her head slowly.

Rapper reached down to his side instinctively, feeling for a weapon of any kind. He had none—his pockets were empty. Rapper looked down at his own, drab Viper outfit and his thin body structure and his mouth went dry.

For the first time in his life, Rapper could "feel" his hands were empty. It was weightier than any stick or laser-slicer he had ever grasped. The feeling brought a fleeting thought to Rapper's mind: Had he *really* trusted that much in material weapons all his life?

Rapper didn't have enough time to answer his own question. Slayer began walking forward slowly, stepping onto the floor painting. His eyes were black, cold and heartless. He obviously wasn't coming after another human...just an opponent.

* * *

Above on the catwalk, Valerie shifted from side to side, trying to pull her wrists together behind her back. Her left binding hit a perpendicular bar. She clumsily slid her entire body to the left. As she did, she prayed.

* * *

Rapper prayed, too. The giant Goliath wasn't slowing down and Rapper didn't even have a slingshot. He quickly scanned the ground for a rock...nothing.

"Use the Electroblade!" Strike First shouted out at Rapper. The Superkid looked back angrily.

"I don't *have* the Electroblade!" he cried.

"You do too!" Strike First argued.

Rapper patted his clothing. He didn't have anything with him. Strike First shot Squealer a glance. Squealer looked back at his leader, confused and shrugging his shoulders.

"Where is it then?!" Strike First cried. "I checked before the fight! You took it out of the drawer!"

"I did not!" Rapper shouted back. "I don't know where it is!"

"You lose this and she will never see the light again!" Strike First threatened, pointing to Valerie.

* * *

Valerie moved to the right and bent back.

* * *

Slayer stopped a few feet away from Rapper and grinned. With a whoosh, he pulled his glowing glove up in the air. His right bicep bulged.

"Aaaaarrrrrggggghhhh!" he bellowed. With his full weight, he leapt toward Rapper.

Rapper dove left and dodged the blow, rolling over the picture on the ground. Slayer's gloved fist clashed with the pavement and sparked wildly. Rapper jumped back up. Slayer growled.

"You don't want to do this!" Rapper cried out. "I know

you're as human as I am!" The killer growled again.
"Aren't you?" Rapper questioned.

* * *

There! Valerie was able to press her right hand into the small of her back. Her fingertips wrapped around the tip of the device she had hidden there until just the right time.

* * *

The Vipers and Claws roared. Strike First shouted more threats at Rapper. The Superkid clenched his fists, knowing that sooner or later he had to come against the rock-solid teenager. His eyes stayed steady, but his thoughts trailed to Valerie. With her life on the line he didn't have a choice. He had to fight with everything within him. He hated doing it, but what choice did he have? If he didn't fight the Claw, Strike First would feel no remorse in hurting Valerie. Besides, if he didn't kill the Claw, he would be killed.

Slayer struck forward again, but not before Rapper jumped up and kicked him in the chest. The Claw was knocked back onto the ground. His cape wrapped around him like a cocoon. Rapper flew back from the jolt of impact, lost his balance and hit the ground, too.

* * *

Valerie lost her grip. She adjusted her position and tried again.

* * *

The throbbing that pierced Rapper's leg proved to him just how solid Slayer really was. Sure, Rapper had knocked him down, but he was nowhere close to knocking him out.

Suddenly, amidst a thunder of cheers and jeers, Slayer was above Rapper. The Superkid's eyes widened in surprise and he crawled backward on the floor like a crab in quick flight.

His eyes full of anger, Slayer lashed out and down again with his fist. Rapper anticipated the blow to his head just in time. The electricity gave him a buzz-cut and nicked his ear. A tuft of his hair blew through the air like a flurry of snowflakes.

* * *

There! She got it! Valerie grabbed the hidden item and slowly pulled it up. She held it out behind her back with her right hand and squeezed the handle.

* * *

Squealer was the first to see the blaze of light come from the catwalk. His mouth dropped in surprise and he shouted to Strike First. The Viper leader's face fell as he realized that Jaws/Valerie had been there when he had hidden the knife in the Common Room drawer…before she was caught.

* * *

Rapper cried out as the kick in his side registered. He tried to catch the Claw's feet in his own and sweep him to the ground, but he didn't have the strength.

"Get up!" Slayer grunted. "Take me on, rad!"

Rapper pushed himself up on one knee and then did all he could to stand. A tear blurred his vision. He couldn't lose this fight. He didn't care about himself...but Valerie shouldn't have been in trouble. She didn't do anything wrong. She only cared. Rapper coughed. He wasn't there for his brother...and now he wasn't there for Val.

* * *

Valerie was determined to get away. If she could get free, maybe Rapper could get free and they could both avoid the consequences of life with the Vipers.

Not wasting any time, Valerie pressed the glowing Electroblade to the steel railing to which her chains were bound. Electricity against steel screeched and sparked as the bar gave way, slicing in two. The railing shook violently for a moment. Yes! One wrist was free! The other, bound to another section of the catwalk, was next.

* * *

"Don't do it!" Rapper cried. "You'll regret it for the rest of your life."

"I've done it before!" the Claw spat. "What makes *you* any different?"

"I'm not a Viper!"

The Claw let out a mean chuckle. "Right. You can't hide your mark of loyalty."

"Please, you don't understand!"

"Are you saying you wouldn't kill me if the odds were reversed?"

Rapper couldn't find the answer.

"Sounds like you're definitely a Viper to me," Slayer accused.

* * *

Valerie came down on the next section of the catwalk railing with the Electroblade. She was almost free! The blade cut into the steel again like a welding fire.

ZAP! A sharp spark shot back and bit Valerie's hand. Without time to think, she screamed and let go of the Electroblade. The power turned off and it dropped to the edge of the catwalk, bounced with a "clink!" and tumbled straight down into the arena.

* * *

Rapper looked up when he heard the scream. He jumped back as the blade came spiraling toward him like an old-time kamikaze bomber. It smacked the cement ground hard, handle first, bounced a few times and came to a rest directly between the opponents, exactly in the center of the painted snake's mouth.

* * *

Valerie pulled on her steel binding. The Electroblade hadn't made it all the way through the railing. She wasn't going anywhere.

* * *

Rapper and the Claw both dove for the Electroblade. Rapper still didn't want anything to do with the destructive thing, but he knew he had to get it before Slayer did.

"Aaarrrgggghhh!" Both opponents screamed, coming down on the knife. They smacked heads and Rapper winced in pain. The Claw lost his bearings for a moment and Rapper seized the opportunity. He grabbed the Electroblade and squeezed it tight.

The blade came to life and its light shined off the metal that lined the knuckles on Slayer's glove.

"It's time I made this fight more even!" Rapper exclaimed. He aimed the Electroblade and sliced the electric circuit across his gloved knuckles in two.

"NOOOO!!!!" Slayer shouted in anger as his glove sparked in protest. Immediately, it was useless. Slayer threw it off his hand. It hit the ground and bounced, throwing sparks, but Rapper didn't notice.

His eyes were fixed upon Slayer's hand.

On the side of his hand, between his thumb and his knuckle was a small, luminous, yellow marking. It was a letter "S." Rapper's heart skipped a beat as he realized he had only seen a mark like that once before…

* * *

The memories came flooding back. More vivid this time. Clearer than ever.

He had been around the corner. His brother said he wanted him to stay near, but Rapper wanted to do his own thing—show his independence. He wasn't doing anything wrong…. He was just looking in a shop when he heard the voices. For the first time since it had happened, his mind remembered those voices.

Nick: "Yo, rad, not now. My brother's with me."

Voice: "I don't see any brother with you, Grrr."

Nick: "He's right h—Rapper? …Rapper?! Where you at?"

Voice: "The Vipers sent me to settle a score. Seems you've been wanting out."

Nick: "I gotta get out, rad. You don't understand. I made a mistake."

Voice: "Your only mistake was that you thought the

Vipers were your family."

As the laser shot pierced the cool evening air, Rapper came running around the corner.

"Nick!" he shouted.

His brother crumpled to the ground before him, falling under a dim street light. Rapper looked up to see the shooter slipping away. His eyes focused on the teenager's hand, gripped around a laser gun. On the side of his hand—between his thumb and his knuckle—glowed a small, yellow "S."

"It's for 'Slayer,'" the young teen whispered with a sorrowful expression as he slipped away.

Rapper stood frozen, holding the Electroblade steadily in front of him.

Slayer didn't flinch.

Strike First egged Rapper on.

The Vipers and the Claws shouted their insults and support.

Above, Valerie prayed softly.

Rapper's gaze moved from the shining Electroblade to the destroyed glove beyond it. He knew with a calculated swipe of the weapon the fight could end. He could hear Valerie's voice run through his mind: "Remember, the Lord is your Defender. Put your trust in Him. Trust His Word. He's made you a winner." But Rapper didn't feel much like a winner. Not yet. Not with Valerie bound. Not with her life on the line. Not with Strike First eager to take power. Not with a deadly weapon in his hands...

He had worked so hard—*so hard*—to get rid of this part of his life. He hadn't held a weapon like this in *four* years. He couldn't remember the last time he had been in a physical fight. But had he really changed all that much? Here he was; he had come full circle. He was in a fight, he had a weapon, he was wearing the clothes...and the mark of loyalty was on the back of his neck. A Viper. There was no mistaking it. A snake that strikes quickly... attacks its prey without remorse.

"Take him down!" Strike First ordered. "Do it and you'll change everything!"

The Vipers cheered their agreement.

Rapper could hear his own heartbeat. It sounded like a drum beating beside his ear. Thump...thump...thump...

Slayer dropped to the ground and swept his feet forward, sliding them across Rapper's calves. Caught off guard, Rapper tumbled sideways, but found his ground again quickly. Slayer was back up, too. They were in the same place as before, only now on opposite sides.

"You killed my brother," Rapper stated flatly. His eyes glowed, reflecting the light from the Electroblade.

"Your brother?" Slayer asked gruffly.

"Four years ago. In a dark alley. His call was Grrr. He had no defense. Why did you do it?"

Slayer shook his head. "What difference does it make? I'm not proud of it," Slayer offered.

The Superkid took a slow step sideways. Slayer imitated it, protecting himself.

"I want to know why he died," Rapper explained

through gritted teeth. "He didn't do you any wrong, I'm sure of it."

The Claw nodded. "You're right. He didn't do me any wrong," Slayer admitted. Rapper was surprised at the comment. His eyes widened.

"I was a free agent then," Slayer continued. "I worked for whoever would pay up. The Vipers paid me to do it. He said he wanted to leave. Bad kid, good kid—in a gang, it doesn't make a difference. In a gang, you're either in or out. There's no in between."

"So that's the deal?"

"That's the deal."

Rapper took a few steps back. Again, Slayer imitated him.

"Kill him!" came the cries from each side.

"What was your payment?" Rapper wondered.

Slayer's deep-set eyes blinked slowly.

"They spared the life of my best friend," he whispered. Then he added, "It was after that deal that I decided to become a Claw...because I found out they were the Vipers' greatest enemy."

"Well, guess what, rad," Rapper said, taking a bold step forward. The Vipers cheered. "Seems we're a lot alike. See, right now I have a decision to make." Rapper pointed straight up to Valerie. "You see that girl up there?" he asked. He didn't wait for an answer. "That's one of my best friends. And I've been told that the only way to save her life is to take you out. What do you think about that?"

Rapper lurched forward and slashed the Electroblade at Slayer. The opponent jumped back, narrowly dodging the blow. Slayer ran to the side, but Rapper stayed on his heels.

"Yaaahhh!" Rapper cried. The Claw stepped backward and stepped on the edge of his waving cape. The step yanked his head back and in total shock he crashed backward onto the ground near the center of the mascot painting.

Rapper didn't waste a second. He came down on Slayer's chest with one knee and held his position. Slayer looked up at him, amazed at his sudden drive. Rapper returned the stare. Then, directly above Rapper, on the catwalk, Valerie caught his eye. Slayer's forehead wrinkled. "I understand," he whispered.

"I don't think you do!" Rapper shouted harshly.

The Vipers shouted, "Finish him! Finish him! Finish him!" The Claws stood in stunned silence. David had brought down Goliath.

"Well, I was right about one thing, rad," Slayer choked out.

Rapper looked at him through narrow eyes.
"What's that?"

"You *are* a Viper."

Rapper felt every muscle in his body tighten as he
raised the glowing Electroblade above his head. He angled
it down.

* * *

"Rapper, no!" Valerie shouted, leaping to the edge of
the railing. "Rapper!" She grabbed the railing with
clenched fists.

A drop of blood rolled from the place where the spark
bit her hand moments ago. It rolled to the edge of her fist
and then...

The drop of blood fell.

* * *

Rapper's fists turned white as he squeezed tighter
onto the Electroblade. The blade buzzed louder, growing
even brighter.

Slayer shut his eyes in fearful expectation.

Rapper looked down at the painted snake's eyes staring
back at him from underneath that V'd eyebrow.

Rapper looked up at his own hands around the weapon.

SPLASH!

The thick, single drop of blood exploded on the back of

Rapper's left hand. The sudden redness surprised Rapper. He let go of the blade with his right hand and used it to wipe the blood off the hand still holding the weapon. He opened his right palm and looked at the crimson stain. It reminded him of the blood that was shed for him—the life that Jesus gave so he wouldn't have to be a victim of the world. It was the strongest blood promise of them all.

It only took one drop of that life-giving blood to save the world from sin. *Why do I think it should take more than that to change who I am?* Rapper thought. Jesus did it once...and that's all that was needed. And here Rapper was living as though he needed something more to *completely* change his life...as though what Jesus did wasn't enough.

Suddenly, as the revelation hit, the back of Rapper's neck began to burn with heat—as if a flame was flickering at the base of his head. Rapper grabbed the back of his neck with his hand and held it there trying to dissipate the heat.

Slayer opened his eyes. As his neck quickly cooled, Rapper pulled his hand away and looked at his palm again. He didn't see the blood anymore, but what he did see startled him. A smudged pool of olive green, black, red and brown covered his palm. The permanent tattoo had just, somehow, melted away.

Then it hit him: Squealer had said the tattoo ink was
repelled by blood...and Valerie's blood had just intermin-
gled with it enough to dissolve the image on his neck.

Rapper glanced down at the snake's scrutinizing eyes
once more. Then he grabbed the Electroblade firmly with
both hands again and fixed his opponent in his sight.

"No!" he shouted authoritatively at Slayer. "I am *not*
a Viper!"

"Wha—"

"I know who I am! I am a *Superkid*—and *I follow the
Lord Jesus Christ!* I am pressing on to win the prize God
has for me! I am more than a conqueror! I am an overcomer!
I am a child of God! I no longer live—but the Anointed
One and His Anointing lives in me! You think I should take
your life? You think that would be justice? You think I
should do it to you because you would do it to me?"

Slayer shook his head.

"I say let God be your Judge!" Rapper shouted. He
threw the Electroblade far to the side. The blade turned off
the moment it left his hands. It slid across the pavement.

Rapper moved his knee off Slayer's chest. Slayer
pushed himself up into a leaning position.

"The old me—the Viper I used to be—would hate you,
Slayer," Rapper admitted. "But I don't. I *won't.* What you

did was wrong, but I *choose* to forgive you, rad."

Slayer's face softened. "I...I don't understand. I...I killed your brother." His deep-set eyes blinked in wonderment.

"The fighting has to stop," Rapper pointed out, softer now. "It begins with me. I left the undercity four years ago. Today, it leaves me."

Slayer was silent for a long moment and then mumbled unintelligibly.

"What?" Rapper asked.

"I...I want to get the undercity out of me, too."

The cries and shouts of the gangs faded into the background as he had Rapper's full attention. "That means you'll have to make Jesus your Lord and leave this place," Rapper explained.

"But they'll never let me leave."

"You can get out," Rapper promised. "It may not be easy, but you can do it. I'll help."

"I want to."

Rapper put his hand out and grabbed Slayer's hand. The boys' fists locked and Rapper locked his eyes with Slayer's.

"Let's pray."

"I don't know how."

"Just say what I say. 'Father God, today I give my life to You.'"

Slayer repeated the words with Rapper.

"The identity I've been living is a false one and I don't want it anymore. Today I become a new person. I make Jesus my Lord. I believe that He died and rose again for me. Make me new, Father. I pray in Jesus' Name."

Slayer repeated every word boldly.

"That's it?" Slayer asked when they finished.

"That's it," Rapper assured. "But keeping your life new every day is up to you."

Rapper helped Slayer up and suddenly realized the room had fallen silent.

"What is this?!" Strike First shouted angrily into his head microphone. The words echoed around the room. "Someone has to die!"

"Someone did," Rapper said, nodding to Slayer.

"Anyone wanna dispute it?" Slayer asked loudly, his strong voice echoing through the den. No one stepped forward.

Strike First glared at the Superkid. "So is this the way you want it?" he asked.

Rapper nodded. "It's the way it is."

"Fine, rad. Say goodbye to your friend."

Strike First jumped into the crowd of Vipers and
emerged a moment later on a Serfsled. With a laser gun
in hand, he zipped through the air, over the heads of
Slayer and Rapper. He was going after Valerie.

Rapper knew it would take him too long to run up
to the catwalk—Strike First was already there. The Viper
leader pulled the brakes on the Serfsled and it came to
a quick, midair stop about 25 feet from where Valerie
was bound.

Below, the Superkid glanced around for any ideas, but
he had none.

Strike First leapt from the Serfsled and landed squarely
on the steel catwalk. He bounded forward toward Valerie,
aiming the laser gun straight ahead, fixing his target.

Rapper prayed, "Lord, You are her Defender
and Shield!"

Valerie pulled at her binding. The chain clanked
against the railing. It wouldn't budge.

Strike First shot once and the blast landed beside
Valerie's shoulder. She jumped.

"Noooo!" Rapper cried.

A flash like lightning zipped past Rapper. It was the
Electroblade zinging through the air. Shining brightly, the
blade flew on a straight and even course for the catwalk.

Strike First's eyes widened as he saw it coming.

Strike First jumped back and the blade singed his hand, slashing into the laser weapon, destroying it. The Viper leader fell back against the railing and grabbed on tight for balance.

The Electroblade bounced once in the air and then cracked against the far side of the railing, searing through the metal on impact and dropping off the catwalk.

In an instant, it hit the ground below, blade first, and snapped in two upon impact.

Above, Valerie shouted out, "Noooo!"

The railing, now cut in two places, with the weight of Strike First in the middle, gave way. Valerie pulled and pulled at her constraints, trying to get free, trying to grab Strike First.

It was no use. It happened too fast.

The railing tumbled backward with Strike First holding on tight.

Rapper ran to try and catch the falling leader, despite the trouble he caused, but Slayer grabbed Rapper and pulled him back across the floor with full force.

"It's too heavy!" he cried. "The railing will crush you!"

Rapper shut his eyes as the railing hit the ground with a loud bang on impact.

When he opened his eyes, Rapper's gaze was drawn not to the fallen leader, but to the broken Electroblade handle, lying a few feet away. A thick rubber band was tied around its base giving it the pressure needed to light the blade.

Rapper picked it up and shouted, "Who threw this?! Who threw it?!"

The room was deadly silent. Rapper knew he would never know. Such was life in the undercity.

Twenty-four hours had passed and Rapper sat cross-legged on the ground, staring at the mural being painted on a nearby cement wall. A thin, white face stretched down the wall highlighted with gray eyes and bright, red eyebrows and hair. Two comical fists were coming straight out. Scrawled at the side were the words:

STRIKE FIRST
10.25
LEADER FOR A TIME,
BUT TIMES HAVE CHANGED

The memorial said it well, Rapper thought.

Valerie, still sporting her bleached hair pulled back in a ponytail, took a seat beside her friend.

"What a week," she said, leaning back against the wall. Rapper nodded. He looked at her wrists. They were bruised from the bonds she had worn.

"Sorry about your wrists," Rapper apologized.

Valerie smiled and rubbed her right wrist. "What—this? Are you kidding? All in a day's work."

The two friends sat side by side in silence for several

minutes. Finally, Rapper spoke up. "Hey, we can go to the surface now if you want. I don't mean to keep us away any longer."

"This changed my life, Rapper," Valerie admitted out of the blue.

Rapper's eyebrows leapt up as he wondered, "It changed *your* life?"

"Yeah," Valerie confirmed. "I came here to help you, but I think you helped me."

"How's that?"

"Well, you know, I grew up on Calypso Island and saw all kinds of people in poverty, sickness, hurting...I've always known there were people out there who needed help. I've always looked forward in time and said, 'Hey, one day I wanna go out to the hurting people of the world.' But I don't think I really realized—until I visited the under-city—that I don't have to go too far. Kids right here in town are hurting just as much as any tribe on any island we've ever visited."

Rapper shook his head. "I'm just sorry the hurting had to come to this." He nodded toward the drying memorial.

"When people sin, they earn what sin pays," Valerie observed, remembering Romans 6:23.

Rapper added, "The undercity proves just how true that is."

"Oh! Hey, one of the Vipers just gave me this letter—said it was left outside the main tunnel with your name on it." Valerie handed Rapper a small, white envelope with the word "RAPPER" scrawled on the front in thin, blue ink. Rapper slid his finger under a corner and tore the envelope open. He pulled out a simple, white letter. Valerie glanced over his shoulder as he read the words written in the same, blue ink:

Rapper,

I hope you get this leter. Sorry if this is to late, but I wanted to say thank you for helping me. I don't be long with the vipers. You new it, but I didn't.

I told my dad about the vipers and he didn't get mad like I thawt. He got me help to get out like you said I could get. The police new who to talk to.

One good thing—my mom and dad are talking again. They went to go to church together and I went to. Now I think maybe GOD and Jesus have something they are going to do for us.

*You didn't think I herd, but I did.
Rad's forever.*

Newbie

"How about that," Valerie said, squeezing Rapper's arm.

"How about that," Rapper repeated her words, smiling. He folded up the letter and slid it back into the envelope. "And you know, I was talking to Slayer and he says after he gets help getting out, he wants to come back to the undercity and minister."

"That's what I'm saying," Valerie expressed, tipping her head back and closing her eyes. "The fields are ready. Like the sign says, times have changed. Maybe the Vipers and Claws have ended their fighting, but they still need to hear...and there are so many more..."

A few more moments passed and then Valerie asked, "So what about you?"

"What about me?" Rapper responded, still staring at the big painting of Strike First.

"What are you going to do now?"

"Get some sleep," Rapper said with a yawn. "A lot of it."

"Guys are so deep," Valerie teased.

"Aw, I know what you mean," Rapper defended himself.

"I'm going to change some things. You know, I've been living like I need to be in total control."

"You?"

"Very funny," Rapper said, twisting his mouth into a sideways smile. "Seriously, Val, I guess I just realized that when I made Jesus my Lord, my spirit was made completely new...but my mind and body—they're still the same they ever were. That's where it's up to me. God made me responsible to pray and read His Word. I have to keep reminding myself of what He's done for me. I have to remember who I am now, in Him. I may not look like it to some people, but I *have* been changed. I'm not a Viper. I'm Robert Rapfield, God's son."

Valerie smiled sweetly. "I'm glad that old, false identity of yours is washed away," she said.

Rapper rubbed the back of his neck. After a few moments, the two Superkids sighed at the same time.

Valerie giggled. "C'mon," she said, standing up. "Let's go. I want to get back to Superkid Academy in time for dinner."

Rapper hopped up. They made their way toward the Viper tunnel leading to the surface when Rapper suddenly stopped.

"What's wrong?" Valerie wondered. He was still

rubbing the back of his neck.

"Val, I can't feel my scar."

"What do you mean?"

"I mean, I can't feel my scar!" Rapper shouted in amazement. Valerie grabbed Rapper's head and whirled him around.

"Yow! Be careful! That's my head!"

"Sorry." Valerie peered closely at the back of Rapper's neck. She swatted his hand twice to get it out of the way.

"So?!" Rapper shouted.

Valerie let go and stood in front of her friend smiling. "That theory you told me earlier—about the blood repelling your tattoo—are you sure that's exactly what happened?"

"Well, it made sense...but, you know, there was a sudden heat on my neck..." he trailed off.

Valerie nodded. "Rapper, do you remember that prophecy the Lord gave me for you?"

Slowly, Rapper spoke the prophecy, word for word.

"All rising tongues shall fall as a drop of life descends.
The right Weapon changes what was to what will be.
Wield It well and find your future where your history
begins, Where vices are transformed into debris."

"You'll find your future where your history begins," Valerie repeated. "Your history begins at the Cross. God didn't just give you a new future, Rapper, He gave you a new history, too. Your old history—"

"—has entirely disappeared," Rapper completed her thought, understanding. Second Corinthians 5:17 came to mind. "I'm a new creation. Old things have gone; everything is made new."

Rapper couldn't help but rub the back of his neck time and again as they made their way to the surface above.

The hard cement the Superkids walked on soon turned to soft clay. The dark tunnel gave way to a broad, bright opening, and beyond, Rapper saw the sun rising through thin, wispy clouds. Lemon-yellow and fiery, orange light spread over the city, reminding him more and more of that golden, Calypso Island sun. Behind him, by the Word of God and the blood of Jesus, the scar of four hard years dissipated into the night. And Rapper's new day was about to dawn. He could see it.

Paradise was just over the horizon.

"I'm just glad things are back to normal," Rapper said enthusiastically.

"Here, here," Superkid Paul agreed.

The large Superkid control room on Level 2 was empty except for the Blue Squad. They had assembled together around their mission table to receive their next assignment from their leader, Commander Kellie.

The five Blue Squad friends—Paul, Missy, Rapper, Valerie and Alex—were there along with Techno, the team's official robot. Each of them felt the warmth of being together again...finally. Refreshment at last.

"It's good to be in the same place again," Commander Kellie said with a sweet smile, standing at the head of the purplish table. The Superkids nodded.

"And if that's not enough, my hair even looks good," Missy threw in for effect.

Valerie giggled. "Mine, too. It's finally brown again."

Paul shook his head and grinned. "So what's our next mission?"

Commander Kellie punched a button on a console at her fingertips and a blue screen lit up at the foot of the table. Slowly the picture of a young boy scrolled into view.

"Who's he?" Rapper asked.

"This is Lincoln Furlong. He's 11 years old—and he's missing."

"Oh my," Missy said under her breath. Paul acknowledged her comment with a bob of his eyebrows.

"That's where we come in," the commander explained. "Lincoln's principal found him alone in his parents' apartment after he hadn't attended school for a week. She immediately called social services, but while she was on the phone, he took off out the door with his jacket, his backpack, a tiny bit of money and a photo of his parents. No one has seen him since. Our mission is to find Lincoln."

"Where are his parents?" Missy asked.

"We don't know that either. But finding Lincoln is our first objective."

"A standard search-and-rescue mission," Paul noted.

Commander Kellie nodded. She looked down and punched a few buttons on her datapad. "Now," she said, looking up. "I—"

Commander Kellie gasped. Missy, Valerie and Alex had vanished right before her eyes.

To be continued...

When a young boy **disappears,**
Valerie and Missy **follow** his lead!

Look for *Commander Kellie and the Superkids*_{SM}
novel #10—

The Runaway Mission
by Christopher P.N. Maselli

Prayer for Salvation

Father God, I believe that Jesus is Your Son and that You raised Him from the dead for me. Jesus, I give my life to You. Right now, I make You the Lord of my life and choose to follow You forever. I love You and I know You love me. Thank You, Jesus, for giving me a new life. Thank You for coming into my heart and being my Savior. I am a child of God! Amen.

About the Author

For more than 10 years, **Christopher P. N. Maselli** has been sharing God's Word with kids through fiction. He is the author of more than 30 books including Zonderkidz' *Laptop* series and the *Superkids* Adventures. He is also the founder of TruthPop.com, dedicated to reaching tweens with the Truth through pop culture.

A graduate of Oral Roberts University, Chris lives in Fort Worth, Texas, with his wife, Gena. He is actively involved in his church's *KIDS Church* program, and his hobbies include inline skating, collecting *It's a Wonderful Life* movie memorabilia and "way too much" computing.

Look for these other books in the *Commander Kellie and the Superkids*_{SM} Adventure Series!

World Offices
of Kenneth Copeland Ministries

For more information about KCM and a free
catalog, please write the office nearest you:

Kenneth Copeland Ministries
Fort Worth, Texas 76192-0001

Kenneth Copeland
Locked Bag 2600
Mansfield Delivery Centre
QUEENSLAND 4122
AUSTRALIA

Kenneth Copeland
Post Office Box 15
BATH
BA1 3XN
U.K.

Kenneth Copeland
Private Bag X 909
FONTAINEBLEAU
2032
REPUBLIC OF
SOUTH AFRICA

Kenneth Copeland
Post Office Box 378
Surrey, B.C.
V3T 5B6
CANADA

Kenneth Copeland Ministries
Post Office Box 84
L'VIV 79000
UKRAINE

We're Here for You!

Believer's Voice of Victory **Television Broadcast**

Join Kenneth and Gloria Copeland and the *Believer's
Voice of Victory* broadcasts Monday through Friday and on
Sunday each week, and learn how faith in God's Word can
take your life from ordinary to extraordinary. This teaching
from God's Word is designed to get you where you want to
be—*on top!*

You can catch the *Believer's Voice of Victory* broadcast
on your local, cable or satellite channels.

Check your local listings for times and stations in your area.

Believer's Voice of Victory **Magazine**

Enjoy inspired teaching and encouragement from
Kenneth and Gloria Copeland and guest ministers each
month in the *Believer's Voice of Victory* magazine. Also
included are real-life testimonies of God's miraculous
power and divine intervention in the lives of people just
like you!

It's more than just a magazine—it's a ministry.

To receive a FREE subscription to *Believer's Voice of Victory,* write to:

Kenneth Copeland Ministries
Fort Worth, Texas 76192-0001
Or call:
1-800-600-7395
(7 a.m.-5 p.m. CT)
Or visit our Web site at:
www.kcm.org

If you are writing from outside the U.S., please contact the KCM office nearest you. Addresses for all Kenneth Copeland Ministries offices are listed on the previous pages.